PARALLEL

Claudia Lefeve

*Katherine,
Happy Reading!
xx Claudia*

Sugar Skull Books

Sugar Skull Books

Copyright © 2011, 2014 Second Edition by Claudia Lefeve

Excerpt Paradox Copyright © 2012 by Claudia Lefeve
All Rights Reserved

Cover art by Robin Ludwig Design Inc.

ISBN: 1466232730
ISBN-13: 978-1466232730

Other books by Claudia Lefeve

Novels
Parallel (Travelers Book One)
Paradox (Travelers Book Two)
Paradigm (Travelers Book Three)

Darkly Beings

Novellas
The Fury

Short Stories
Hitched (A Travelers Series Short Story)

*To my high school physics teacher, Juan Ybarra (aka Dad),
who always said science and math weren't my thing.*

"listen: there's a hell of a good universe next door; let's go"
e.e. cummings

Prologue
Miller High Life and Pall Malls

Like any orphan, I wished that someday my real family would come for me. Only, I knew my parents were dead. They died in a plane crash when I was five. But in my dreams, I always imagined my rescue from foster care, I'd learn I was really a princess, and we'd live happily ever after.

Like most daydreams, they'd quickly dissipate and I'd jump back to reality, remembering who and where I was— an orphan stuck with Lester and Patsy Johnson—along with six other foster kids.

If you asked around town, most folks would consider seven abandoned kids lucky to be under the care of the Johnson's. There weren't many couples who were willing to open their home to care for our sorry lot. What they didn't know was that we kept the Johnson's finances afloat. To them, being foster parents was easier than applying for food stamps.

But as self-righteous as the other families around town were, nestled in their idealistic homes and raising perfect children of their own, they were blind to what was really going on behind the Johnson's closed doors. The attention they lavished on their wards wasn't exactly the type the foster care system approved of, nor the good citizens of Alexandria—had their gaze extended beyond their casual observance around town.

Lester was a sadist. To fulfill his penchant for violence, he exploited the revolving turnover of foster kids to satisfy his warped need to inflict pain. His wife Patsy was no better. She was just that—a patsy. She merely took care of the house and turned a blind eye when it came to Lester's extracurricular activities. She was all too happy to play Betty Crocker, as long as Lester had his attention focused on anyone other than herself.

"Emily! Get down here!" We heard him call from downstairs.

I watched Emily's face crumple as Lester called her down to the basement. That's where he always took us. She was only seven years old and was no match for Lester, even on his bad days. He always came up with some house infraction—like the time he claimed I didn't take out the trash—and used that as an excuse to beat us until he was satisfied.

"It'll be okay Emily." I looked at her sad brown eyes. "I'll walk down with you." What I really wanted to do was take Emily and run.

"Etta, I didn't do anything, I swear," she said in a whimper.

My heart went out to her. How do you explain to a seven year old that men like Lester didn't need an excuse?

Claudia Lefeve

"I know you didn't, honey," I said, unsure of what to do next. Ignoring Lester just made things go from bad to worse. I had taken up residence in the Johnson home only two weeks ago—I was what social services dubbed a 'repeat customer'—but it didn't take long to realize that Lester preferred the younger kids who couldn't fight back. I only had the pleasure of dealing with Lester a couple of times, but I knew that the longer you took to respond the worse off you'd be.

Inside, my body seethed with rage. How could the social workers turn a blind eye to what was going on? Didn't they notice the bruises and broken spirits when they were thrown back into their custody? Having played the system for years, Lester knew exactly what he was doing and took great care not to send the children back with tell-tale marks, but sometimes it was unavoidable. And yes, when Lester tired of a particular child and the foster kid got a bit older, he'd thrust them right back to the disgruntled, underpaid, and overworked social workers.

So the faster I got Emily to the main floor, the better off her punishment—if you could call it that—would be.

I reluctantly hustled her down the stairs and there stood Lester, standing at the foot of the stairs, waiting for her. If I'd had the guts, I would have kept on right past him—out the front door.

"Well, well. What do we have here, huh? Looks like someone's meddling in other people's business again." Lester was not only nasty on the inside, but on the outside as well. His beer belly did nothing to help his already oafish build. Every time he managed to get close to me, I could smell his rotten breath mixed with a hint of Miller High Life and stale Pall Malls.

As we reached the foot of the stairs, he pulled Emily from my protective hold, forcing her to release my hand, and led her toward the side of the stairwell towards the basement door. It tore me up, watching Emily being dragged down the basement stairs, to the point where I felt numb. There was nothing I could do for her.

"You're next girl," he sneered back at me.

It was as if I were frozen, knowing what was about to happen, and being powerless to stop him. I couldn't tear myself away from the open doorway, continuing to watch as Lester and Emily descended down the stairs, with his oil stained mechanic's hand cupping Emily's back, ushering her ahead of him.

That's when I finally snapped.

"Let go of her," I yelled at the top of my lungs. *Stop, stop, stop!* I continued to scream in my head.

"What did you say girl?" Lester stopped mid-stair and released his hold on Emily. He walked back up the staircase and glared up at me with his beady little eyes. He really did look like an oversized troll. "What did you say?"

"I said, let her go you fat ogre." I couldn't control myself.

STOP, STOP, STOP! The voice in my head was getting louder and louder.

"Why you little—" Lester started to say. He tried to reach for me and then, just as quickly as he had climbed up the stairs, he began to clutch his heart and fell backwards down the stairs.

"Emily! Watch out!" I yelled.

Claudia Lefeve

Chapter One
Dominion House for Girls

I'm standing in the middle of my new room and can't help but wonder for the millionth time how I ended up here. The walls are constructed out of cinderblocks, coated with glossy white paint, waiting for its new occupants to mar them up with tacky celebrity posters and bulletin boards. A pair of twin beds line up against two of the walls that lie parallel to each other. With a set of desks and an adjoining bathroom connecting to the suite next door, this place isn't too shabby as far as dorm rooms go. Only, it isn't really a dorm. That's just what the administrators prefer to call the small twelve by twelve rooms. Still, my last foster home was with the Johnson's, so this is a definite improvement.

Dominion House for Girls is considered the last resort when it comes to foster kids that nobody wants to deal with. The institution-like structure is meant to give the impression of a boarding school, when in fact it's more akin to a correctional facility for troublemakers. My only concern is my new roommate. I just hope I don't get stuck with someone with a worse temperament than me.

❄

When I was about ten, I'd been dumped with the Clark family. Their daughter Maxine was thirteen and she had taken a special interest in me. And not in a sisterly way either; the girl couldn't stop bullying me. If there was anyone spoiled and screwed up in that house, it was Maxine.

Once a month, the Clarks met with several of the neighbors for a potluck dinner. Normally, they hired a sitter to watch over me and Maxine, but on that particular night they decided Maxine was old enough to babysit. This was the opportunity she'd been waiting for and the moment I dreaded. When I stubbornly decided not to go to bed—a decision I now regret—she began to chase me around the living room and had me cornered up against the wall.

"I'm not going to hurt you. I swear." Her eyes twinkled. "I just want to play."

"Leave me alone." I'd already had the pleasure of playing with her before and the only one it was ever fun for was Maxine.

"Come on Etta. If you don't, I'll tell mom and dad," she said. Any time I refused to play one of her little games, she would vandalize something in the house and blame it on me.

"If you come near me, I'll tell them that you were the one that cut my hair!" The week prior, she'd snuck into my room when I was sleeping and cut a big chunk of my hair off. I knew Mrs. Clark wouldn't believe that her precious daughter was the one responsible, so I lied and told her I got gum stuck in hair and decided to cut it out myself.

"Yeah right dork, like they're really gonna believe you over me," she said.

Maxine had a point.

She had me backed up against the corner, leaving me without a means to escape. That's when I realized I had been holding my breath and I let it all out in one big whoosh. *Just leave me alone!*

Maxine slowly crept her way towards me as I kept chanting in my head, *just go away, leave me alone!*

With every step she took, I increased my chant. Over and over I wished for her to stop. And as quickly as she began her hunt, she suddenly stopped in her tracks. Her legs gave out and she tripped over the living room rug, hitting her head on the corner of the coffee table.

As hurt as she was, she didn't waste any time running next door to snitch on me, leaving behind a bloody trail that ran from the coffee table in the living room out the front door. According to Maxine's version of events, I had pushed her up against the coffee table for not allowing me to stay up past bedtime. The following day, the social worker had been contacted and I had been farmed out to yet another foster home.

At ten years old, I didn't know if I was lucky or cursed.

❀

Unlike a lot of foster kids, I'm not what most people would consider a head case. With Alexandria located only a couple of minutes away from Washington, D.C., the sins of the city overflow into the Commonwealth of Virginia, resulting in a ton of neglected children due to crackhead moms, parents slain in drive-by shootings, or dads taking up residence at the county jail. Sometimes, they end up in foster care simply because they're too much for their folks to handle. Things like that can really screw-up a kid.

According to my file, I'm saddled with the labels of both orphan and difficult. It isn't intentional I just have the unfortunate pleasure of being present whenever people get hurt—like little Maxine. Incidents are either chalked up to accidents or blamed on me. Either way, I always get passed off to another family within the system.

After the episode with Lester, I learned from one of the social workers that he'd suffered a heart attack and ultimately broke his neck when he went barreling down the stairs. The police would later say Lester got off easy, which left Patsy facing seven counts of child abuse and some serious jail time. But at fifteen, no one was eager to take on a girl with 'violent tendencies', so I ended up at Dominion House.

When I first arrived at Dominion two years ago, I had to share a room with three other girls in tiny bunk style quarters not much larger than a shoebox. Now that I'm seventeen, I'm considered a last year resident. The only perks that come with this distinction is a new dorm assignment, which means a bigger room (but not by much), and a new roommate. For her sake, I hope she's easy to get along with. I managed to spend the last two years without any major mishaps. Sure, I got into some scuffles—just like prison, there's a hierarchy to maintain here—but nothing near as bad as what I did to Lester.

Being the first to occupy the room, I settled in with high expectations for a fresh start. I only pray my roommate won't mind that I already staked my claim on the

Claudia Lefeve

bed by the window. Sometimes, when I can't sleep, I like to look out the window and gaze up at the stars. But I imagine it will be a small concession on her part, as I left her plenty of closet space. Despite what others might think about foster kids and our proximity to the nation's capital, Northern Virginia is still one of the wealthiest areas in the country, rivaled only by the suburbs of New York City. So it's not unusual for many of the girls that enter Dominion to have a lot of personal effects, handed down by previous foster families.

As I lay on my bed, imagining for the millionth time all the possible scenarios in which my parents could have survived that plane crash, I hear a soft knock on the door. Almost immediately, I recognize the glorious platinum blonde hair as my new roommate strolls in. She's even more gorgeous now than when I last laid eyes on her. Not that I'm jealous—I'm merely stating the facts.

"Jaime?" I can't believe my luck. The odds of her walking through that door were pretty slim. Not only do I have a new room assignment that doesn't involve a power play for the top bunk, but I actually get paired with a friend. Looks like my last year here is going to be much more tolerable than I first imagined.

"Etta, I can't believe it!" Jaime drops her worn hand-me-down bag at the door and runs towards me. Her bear hug gives me a chance to fully breathe in her scent. It reminds me of cotton candy.

"What are you doing here?" I hold my old friend at arm's length, giving her the once over. "I can't believe it either."

Jaime smiles and proceeds to hug me all over again.

"I've always wondered what happened to you. I missed you so much after you left. I'm glad you haven't forgotten about me."

It's hard to forget a girl like Jaime. "It's been like what, four years?" I'm almost eighteen, so if you want to get technical, it was more like three and a half years ago. "What happened to the Thornberry's?" From what I remember, the family that fostered us several years ago had been stuffy and boring. "I thought you'd have been adopted by now."

Oliver and Melissa Thornberry were an affluent family that couldn't have children of their own. Because Mr. Thornberry was a major political player in Washington, they figured fostering a couple of kids would boost their public image and appeal to voters by appearing more family oriented. Once it became clear I was a potential liability, they sent me packing and kept Jaime.

Jaime snickers. "Oh, Melissa pulled a Martha Stewart and got busted for insider trading. Oliver was only too happy to send me back once he realized his own wife would be housed by the state. When his personal life became tarnished, I wasn't such a political asset anymore."

Yup, this is the same Jaime I so envied and loved.

Jaime's giggle is infectious and I can't help but laugh right along with her. "I guess I shouldn't feel guilty about planting stink bombs in their toilet then." Not only did that period mark the beginning of my teen years, it was also around the time I had a fascination with pranks—explosives to be more exact. And that my friends, is how I got kicked out of the Thornberry house after just two months.

"Well, you certainly made an impression, that's for sure." Jaime hops on the bed I'd already appropriated for myself. "This is great! We have so much to catch up on."

And just when I thought I wouldn't have to fight for a bed. *Please don't be claiming that bed as your own.*

But in the end I was right. Jaime is so ecstatic about having a closet almost entirely to herself that she doesn't even complain about my claiming the bed by the window. After arranging all her clothes, she plops herself onto the bed (her own this time), and we end up sitting across the room from each other, trying to come up with something to say.

I'm relieved that Jaime turned out to be my roommate, but we'd only really known each other for a couple of months before the Thornberry's kicked me out. God, it seemed like ages ago. It's doubtful we have very much to catch up on, but if I want to survive my last year here, I have to remember that she's not only an old friend, but an ally. It's us against the system.

Three and a half years is a long time between friends, so I don't know just how much she's actually changed, but Jaime seems harmless enough. There doesn't seem to be any indications of any harmful side effects from living with a highly influential family like the Thornberry's. She could have turned out differently—like a spoiled rich bitch. But instead, she's the same old beautiful bubbly girl I remember from when I was fourteen.

We spend the remainder of the night catching up, gabbing about what's gone on in our lives over the last four years. Jaime goes on and on about going to college next year and all the cute boys she's going to meet, while I avoid the topic all together—college is out of the question for me.

Instead, I tell her about my exploits, moving around from home to home. Somewhere in the conversation, I realize she managed to live a pretty normal life, while mine seems to mirror the life of a hobo.

It's almost two in the morning by the time we finally fall asleep. My daydreams begin to invade my subconscious and I welcome the reoccurring dreams that invade my sleep each night. I live in a beautiful two story colonial where I have my own bedroom. Sometimes the scenes vary, but they always take place in the same house.

In tonight's episode, my father and I are in the kitchen laughing over a plate of heavenly lasagna. A woman I don't recognize is also there and she's happy that we are all together, enjoying the home cooked meal she's prepared.

The dream sequences have become pretty commonplace the last couple of weeks. I don't know why I keep dreaming of the same people night after night, but I'm not complaining. If I can't be part of a family in real life, at least I can imagine myself in a world where I do—even if it's only in my dreams.

Claudia Lefeve

Chapter Two
Battle Grounds

Dominion House for Girls is located right inside the Alexandria city limits and is funded by generous donations supplemented by the Commonwealth of Virginia. Thus, Dominion operates a bit differently than other state run institutions. Even though the donors like to consider this a progressive institution, the place is nothing more than a gilded probation house. The board that runs the facility consists of private benefactors who believe in keeping positive appearances—so they can have something to brag about at their fancy country clubs—which is why Dominion House is fashioned more like a boarding school than a foster care facility. Heaven forbid we give the impression we are anything other than aberrant foster kids. So, due to their desire to maintain a respectable public image, we're allowed to leave the grounds during limited hours, attend public school, and some of the girls are even allowed to maintain their own personal funds, if they have any.

Like Jaime. She's one of the fortunate ones who actually has access to money. Her parents died when she was six, making her an orphan like me and leaving her with a sizable trust, unlike me. When she lived with the Thornberry's, she even attended one of the local private schools in the area—she had to pay her own tuition of course. To this day, I can't understand why Jaime doesn't take advantage of all her money and go to a real boarding school. Anything has to be better than this dump. It's no wonder she went on and on the other night about going to college. She can afford to go.

Dominion House is conveniently situated near the local high school, so those of us that don't have emotional or behavioral disabilities are allowed to leave the grounds and attend Alexandria High. Apparently, my being labeled delinquent doesn't qualify me for in-house instruction. Not that I mind. For the eight hours that I get to leave the grounds, I feel like a normal teenage girl.

After class, I drag myself back to our room and find Jaime propped up on her bed typing away on her laptop. Personal funds are overseen by designated trustees, but we can purchase things like computers or books for educational purposes. I don't have the means for something like a laptop so I have to rely on the library if I want to do research or check emails. Not that I have anyone emailing me—unless you count spam. I mumble a weak greeting to Jaime, drop my books at my desk, and sprawl on top of my bed.

At first I ignore it, but Jaime's stares get the better of me. "What?" I finally ask. I know it's not like she's purposely trying to be rude, but her staring is starting to get on my nerves.

Jaime laughs the way all beautiful girls do: hearty and confident. "Nothing silly. I don't know what I would have done if I had to come back to all this without you around." She waves her hand around to indicate the glumness of the room.

"I guess," I say, not knowing how else to respond. Jaime is a quite a sight, sitting on her bed, all bouncy and perky, while I'm just, well, me. I don't get exactly why she's acting thrilled about the situation. Don't get me wrong, I'm happy to finally have a friend around here, but it's not like we're tragic characters in a Charles Dickens tale. I mean, being an orphan sucks and all, but hey, that's life.

"Hey, we've been stuck in the dorms every night this week," Jaime says as she slides the laptop off her lap. "Why don't we go somewhere else to study for a change?"

"I don't see how the library can be any more scintillating than this." I really don't want to walk all the way to the public library. It's a twenty minute walk each way and I can spend that time doing something more productive, like watching a repeat episode of <u>Fringe</u>.

"No, I mean, let's go get some coffee or something."

Not only is owning my own laptop out of the question, but so is a simple cup of Joe. Even before I came to Dominion House, I had to save my pennies. It's not like I have a trust that doles out an allowance every week—like someone else I know. Maybe I was a bit rash in dismissing the library. At least there, the books are free.

Jaime must have picked up on my hesitation. "My treat of course. You look like you could use a grande-double-mocha."

I have no idea what the hell that is, but I'm not going to let on that I don't.

Crap. This leaves me with two options: I can be proud and decline or accept her offer and be gracious. In the end, I cave. "Sure, it'd be nice to get out of here for awhile." It's just a cup of coffee, right?

"Great!" She grinned. "Let's go to Battle Grounds."

Both Dominion House and the coffee shop are located within the historic section of Alexandria, better known as Old Town, but it still takes us fifteen minutes to get there on foot. Battle Grounds got its name due to its close proximity to the statue of the Confederate soldier on the corner of Washington and Prince Streets. The soldier doesn't have a name, so it's simply known as The Confederate Statue. I guess the proprietors of the coffee shop wanted to keep with the theme of the block, even though a Civil War battle never occurred here—at least not to my knowledge. The shop is actually a renovated old colonial style townhome that most likely served as a family homestead before the surrounding area was slowly eaten up by the ever growing population. It isn't a large building, but it has a balcony off the second story, and the shop fits in well amongst the other historical buildings along the drag.

We haven't even placed our order when Jaime leaves me in charge of holding our place in line as she goes in search of a bathroom. The aroma of the coffee is so intoxicating that I'm glad Jaime convinced me to come. I wait patiently for the girl ahead of me to order a triple-chai-soy-machiado-whip drink.

And I thought Jaime was weird talking about grande-mocha-whatever's.

I hear a deep chuckle coming from the other side of the shop. That's when I notice him across the room, looking directly at me. He's darkly handsome in a rugged kind of way. The guy definitely isn't someone I recognize from around town. Granted, I hardly notice people, but it's not like we live in a big city. One of the advantages of living so close to Old Town is the small-town feel. Not to mention that Battle Grounds is where you'll find most of the locals, while tourists prefer the predictability of the Starbucks located on the other end of King Street. Then again, its springtime and we always have an abundance of visitors this time of year. He's probably a tourist who stumbled upon the coffee shop hoping to warm up after being out in the brisk cold air.

My attention goes back to the barista, silently wishing she would hurry up on the drink orders. But my curiosity gets the better of me and I chance another look at the stranger. Bummer. He isn't standing across the room anymore and I don't want to give the impression I'm searching for him, so I don't scan the area for signs of him. Besides, they probably already called his order and he took off.

Tired of waiting in line, I decide to ditch it and go in search of Jaime instead. The chick behind the counter is taking way too long to pour coffee and I'm annoyed at this point. If Jaime really wants a drink, she can wait herself.

I find myself going up to the second floor and I check inside the women's bathroom. I peek under each of the two stalls and find them both empty. Then, after a quick search of the second floor lounge area, I make my way back down the winding staircase and accidentally bump into the same guy I had been ogling from across the room. He's standing right at the foot of the staircase, blocking my path back to the main section of the café. I guess he didn't leave after all.

"I saw you get out of line. I hope you don't mind." He waves a second cup of coffee in my direction. "I didn't know how you liked it prepared, so I made sure they left a little room for cream."

The guy is even more gorgeous up close and personal. His weathered jeans and untucked white button-down gives him a rough and masculine appearance. The stark black eyes that gaze into mine clash against the rest of his features; his sandy blond hair almost demands he have blue ones. I stand there for several seconds, not being able to stop myself from staring back into his eyes. Reluctantly, I snap back from his gaze and notice he's actually offering me the cup of coffee. I can actually feel my entire face turn red with embarrassment.

"Are you sure that's not for someone else?" He probably bought that second cup for a friend, and then decided to give it to me at the last minute. It's hard for me to imagine anyone being that nice. In my experience, people don't go out of their way to do thoughtful things—at least that's what I learned from the folks I grew up around.

I can't seem to move from my current position. It's almost as if his body gives off these little electronic waves that flow directly into my own. I can feel the goose bumps on my arms as I continue to stare up at him like a grade-A dork. This is the kind of thing that happens to good looking girls like Jaime, who are prepared for these types of social interactions, not someone like me. Don't get me wrong, I'm not self-conscious about my appearance that I consider myself unattractive—that's for girls who lack self-confidence. I'm just plain. My long brown hair lacks luster and my brown eyes are neither exotically dark nor light like

Claudia Lefeve

toffee. Not that I care, but at this moment, I wish I was more like Jaime when it comes to the looks department.

"Nope. It's all yours." He hands me the tall cup of coffee. "Shall we?" He motions to one of the empty tables up at the front of the shop near the windows. Normally, I don't make it a habit of taking drinks from complete strangers, nor accepting invitations to accompany them, but with Jaime still missing, I figure I can kill some time before she comes back.

Sitting opposite each other, I'm able to get a better look at him. He looks older than the guys I go to high school with and if I have to guess, I'd say he's around twenty, twenty-one. At the very least, he definitely appears more mature than any of the other guys I've come across at school.

"So, do you want some cream or sugar?" He offers.

"No, I'm good." The fragrant smell generating from the steaming hot cup tells me I don't need to sully it with added crap.

"I'm Cooper." He grins, flashing a perfect set of teeth. He probably never had to wear braces and will never need to spend a dime on tooth whitening strips. His smile is that flawless.

"Etta." I extend my hand to shake his. "Thanks for the coffee. Um, I'm actually here with a friend, I just don't know where she ran off to." Single girl survival tip 101: always let strange men know you're not alone. This way they know not to try anything stupid like slipping roofies in your drink. Okay, I know we're in a coffee shop, but a girl can't be too careful.

"If you're talking about that blonde you came in with, I'm sure she got sidetracked talking to some guy."

Great. I'm sure he's only sucking up to me so I can later introduce him to Jaime. I got so caught up talking with him that I didn't stop to question why a good looking guy like him would buy a girl like me a cup of coffee.

"You're probably right." This isn't the first time Jaime's forsaken me for someone she just met.

I feel a big tug on my right elbow. Speak of the devil— I turn just in time to see Jaime looking beyond annoyed. "Hey, where'd you run off to? I was looking for you." Now that I'm talking to Cooper, I wish she'd stayed where she was.

"What are you doing here?" She hisses.

At first, I think she's addressing me, but one look at her face indicates her irritation is aimed directly at Cooper. Does she know him? I'm sure Jaime would have mentioned knowing him. Taking a protective stance, her hand moves from my elbow to my shoulder.

"It's a free country, darlin'. I can support any establishment I want." He counters back. Unlike Jaime, he seems to be enjoying this.

We've been sitting for several minutes and this is the first time I notice the drawl in his voice. Perhaps he's one of those people whose Southernisms come out when they're drunk, provoked, or in this instance, amused.

"Hey, Jaime, I'm—" I try to break away from her hold, but this only tightens her grip on my shoulder.

"Come on Etta, we're leaving." Jaime attempts to drag me out of the place. From the look in her eyes, she is hell bent and determined to get me out of here, even if it means dislocating my shoulder. This isn't good. She must know him or she wouldn't be acting this way.

Claudia Lefeve

"What? Why? I don't understand." Confused, I look over at Cooper. He doesn't make an effort to move from his seat and watches as Jaime pulls me out of the chair, clearly entertained by the spectacle we are no doubt creating.

Jaime looks him square in the eye. "You need to go back to wherever it is you came from."

"Why don't we just let Etta decide?" His attention shifts from Jaime over to me. "Etta, do you want to leave or do you want to stay here and talk? Don't let her bully you into anything."

A small crowd begins to gather where the three of us are arguing. Again, this isn't good. The familiar feeling of my blood pressure rising is never a good sign and I don't know what's going to happen if I end up getting upset. Will my temper affect Jaime or Cooper? It's not like I can control whatever it is I have. I don't even know how it works. All I know is that any time I get upset or felt threatened, bad things happen. What if I get angry and I inadvertently hurt someone? I'm not willing to take any chances.

I don't want to cause an impending scene, so I decide to go along with Jaime and leave. I'm not thrilled with her telling me what to do, and I still think she's taking things a little too seriously, but this Cooper guy must be an ex-boyfriend or they wouldn't be going at each other this way. Jaime and I have to get out now. The situation is getting way out of control, not to mention my body temperature.

"Come on Jaime, you win, we're going now." I grab hold of her hand, allowing her to lead me out of the shop. As we make our way out, I can't help but peer over my shoulder to look at Cooper one last time. Instead of being annoyed that our conversation was cut short, he still has the same amused expression on his face. I silently mouth, "I'm sorry," and follow Jaime out the door.

After all my reservations about going to Battle Grounds, I'm kinda bummed to be leaving. Jaime has some major explaining to do when we get back to Dominion House.

"We have to get out of here now before he follows us."

"I don't think it's going to come to that. When we get back, you're going to tell me exactly what all that was about."

My statement catches catch her off guard, as if she hasn't thought past getting me out of the coffee shop. "I'll explain when we're safe back at the home."

When we get back to our room, Jaime places herself in the middle of her twin sized bed. She glances around the room and then back at me. "I'm so sorry, Etta. I shouldn't have left you alone," she says.

"Yeah, about that. Where did you go? Cooper and I were just talking anyway. I don't see what the big deal was. Why were you acting so weird back there?"

"I'm sorry I left you there all alone. I bumped into Bridgette on my way to the bathroom and got sidetracked," Jaime explains. "Look, I wish we could avoid this conversation all together, but there's something you need to know."

When I think back to all that had transpired tonight, there's nothing that could have prepared me for what Jaime says next.

"That guy you were talking to at the coffee shop? He's been around here."

Claudia Lefeve

Chapter Three
Alexandria High

"What...?" For a second I misunderstand and think Jaime is saying she's seen him around town. But that doesn't make any sense. So, I'm pretty sure she means here at Dominion House.

"You heard me. He came by asking for you," Jaime continues. "And somehow he manages to track you down over at Battle Grounds? That's not good Etta. One minute he's here snooping around, asking if I know you, and the next thing I know, you're all cozied up with him at the coffee shop."

"Did he say why?" Granted, our interaction was brief, but he probably would have gotten around to telling me why he was looking for me if Jaime hadn't intervened. There has to be a reasonable explanation. "And for your information, I wasn't all cozied up. We were just talking. He was nice enough to get me a cup of coffee. I got tired of waiting for you."

"No, he didn't say why. That's why I got you out of there." She says this with a serious tone in her voice. "What if he's some kind of a stalker?" Her face softens a bit. "Look, I'm sorry I left you there alone. I didn't think I'd be chatting that long."

What Jaime said makes sense, but I'm still not willing to buy the fact that Cooper could be dangerous. I want to give Jaime the benefit of the doubt, but she's seriously overreacting about the whole thing and paranoia isn't my idea of a good character trait in a friend—or a roommate. I hope I'm not expected to live my last year at Dominion House with a total control freak. She's my friend, sure, but in the end, I have to look out for myself.

Jaime must realize how ridiculous she sounds and relaxes on the bed. "It's just freaky, that's all. Sorry if I went a little overboard back there. You can't be too safe nowadays."

"You're probably right. It is kinda weird," I say as a way of calling a truce. But in the back of my mind, I didn't think it was weird at all and I can't get the image of his perfect smile out of my head.

Then again, if Cooper is going around asking about me, why didn't he just tell me that back at Battle Grounds? And how did he know to ask for me here at Dominion House? It just doesn't add up. I can't think of a possible reason for him to come looking for me.

Unless... "Hey, do you think..." I know I'm letting my imagination get the better of me, but my thoughts come stumbling out, "...do you think maybe he's some sort of relative or something?"

Jaime springs up from bed with a wide-eyed expression. I can tell she looks sorry for me. "Oh, Etta. I

Claudia Lefeve

don't think so. If that was the reason, don't you think he would have said so from the start?" She then turns away from me and faces the wall. "You know, I have thoughts like that too. That some long lost family member will realize I'm in this hell-hole and take me home."

I can hear her sniffle under the sheets and I realize I'm not the only one who daydreams about being reunited with a family that simply doesn't exist. I know it's a long shot, but why can't it be possible? "Yeah, you're probably right," I finally agree and turned over in my bed, staring back at my own barren side of the wall.

Tonight, I dream about going to a fancy ball. I'm wearing a knee-length silver formal and I feel like a princess. I can't tell who my date is, but I'm positive he's cute.

⚛

At school, I try to keep thoughts of Cooper and his mysterious appearance into my life out of my head. A small part of me still holds on to the belief that he's here to tell me I have family out there—waiting for me to come home. But I know Jaime's right. If that's the case, he would have gone straight to the administration office to discuss the matter.

"Miss Fleming, are you still with us the morning?"

"Sorry, Mr. Duncan." I'm a bit embarrassed at being caught daydreaming in English class. Mr. Duncan is one of my favorite teachers and the last thing I want is for him to think I don't care about his class.

Jaime is in the same class and she leans over her desk to poke me when Mr. Duncan isn't looking. "Hey, are you okay?"

"Yeah," I whisper back. I don't want to tell her I'm thinking about Cooper. She'll give me another lecture for sure. I settle back into my chair and listen attentively to Mr. Duncan's lecture on Shakespeare's *A Midsummer Night's Dream* for the remainder of class.

As soon as the bell rings, Jaime and I hightail it to the cafeteria, which is the only time we get to hang out during the day—as if sharing a room back at Dominion isn't enough face time. But since English is the only class we share together, we take advantage of the lunch hour and spend it catching up on idle gossip.

"So, did you hear, Amy Pierce is preggers," Jaime says in a hushed voice. I don't know why she bothers to whisper. There's no one else at our table to overhear our conversation. Because we're orphans and live over at Dominion House, it pretty much seals our fate as social pariahs at school.

"Really? I thought she was all religious and stuff." Then again, isn't it always the pious ones? Amy is president of the Bible Fellowship Youth Ministry and spent the latter part of last year trying to convert all of us heathens. By the time she got to me, I told her I was Catholic and didn't need to be saved. I don't actually know what I am, but I figured that would shut her up. It didn't though. After that, she and her ministry pledged to save my soul. The finally gave up last semester after their group was nominated to head up the high school's beautification project.

"Pretty sure. Bridgette all but confirmed it the other night at Battle Grounds."

"Well, it could be worse, it could be us," I laugh. People always think the worst about foster kids.

Claudia Lefeve

"Speaking of, do you think Alex would notice us if we weren't orphans?" Jaime slides her lunch tray across the table, eyes focusing on the table situated at the other end of the cafeteria.

I guess even girls like Jaime have confidence issues. I follow the direction of her gaze and immediately understand the reason behind her question. The back corner table is where all popular kids sit, including Alex Stewart. Not only is he captain of the football team, he also dates the most popular girl at Alexandria High, Jenny Prado. And I'd be remiss if I didn't point out, she's captain of the cheerleading team—but do I really have to say it?

"How are those two topics even related? And to answer your question, no." I go back to munching on a french fry. Hamburger Day at school is my favorite day of the week. They actually use real meat for their burgers, not the crap ones filled with fillers, like the ones they serve us over at Dominion House. "We'd have to be cheerleaders too. It's in the teenage handbook. Even then, I'm not sure we'd have a shot."

Jaime sighs. "I know. Just wondering out loud."

"Uh, huh." I lose interest in my soggy fry and look up at Jaime. "You know, we're almost outta here. We'll be eighteen soon and you'll probably be going off to college. I don't know what I'll be doing, but my point is, it's a chance for us to start over. You know, be whoever we want to be."

She stops staring at the table across the cafeteria and immediately brightens up. "A new beginning. I like that."

The bell rings, signaling the end of lunch. Jaime and I pick up our empty trays to deposit on the conveyor on our way out, when I feel a shove on my right side. It's too hard for it to be an accident, so I immediately get in defense mode. "Hey."

"Sooo sorry." A hollow laugh follows Jenny's snide apology. "Didn't see you there."

"Sure you didn't." I glance over Jenny's head just in time to see Alex's apologetic expression. I raise my eyes in response, as if to say, "nice girlfriend you got there." It never ceases to amaze me when guys overlook bitchiness in favor of looks.

"Come on Etta, we don't want to be late for class." Jaime pulls me away from a scene I'm not entirely sure I want to avoid. Ever since I enrolled at Alexandria High, Jenny has had it in for me and I can't understand why. Okay, I can. I'm a nobody in her eyes, so in her world, it's okay to pick on the poor orphan girl. And she's the one with the rich parents, fancy car, and most importantly, Alex. Just once, I'd like to show her a piece of my mind.

Chapter Four
The Storm Trooper

In the days that follow, the incident at Battle Grounds is long forgotten. Actually, it's more like we don't discuss it. Whatever thoughts about Cooper I have, I keep to myself. I'm still not going to confide in Jaime that I can't stop thinking about him.

After another boring day at school, I decide to clear my head. Instead of going straight back to the dorms, I end up going for a walk. Jaime has her weekly counseling session with the in-house social worker, so I don't have to answer any questions about where I'm going. All the girls at Dominion have to undergo weekly sessions—which is a complete waste of time if you ask me. All my counselor wants to do is focus on is why I have these aggressive tendencies. Right, like I'm going to tell her it's all in my mind—literally.

The late afternoon breeze makes it much cooler than usual, so I throw on a light jacket before I head out. I'm not exactly sure where I'm headed, but I don't want to get caught without something to keep myself warm during my walk. The administrators have somewhat flexible rules for those of us over sixteen. We're allowed to leave the confines of Dominion House, as long as we are back by our eight o'clock curfew.

After walking around for several minutes, I realize I'm headed straight to Battle Grounds. I quickly check to see how much money I have on me—about three bucks. I don't want to loiter inside without buying anything. At least it's enough to get me a small regular coffee and refills are free.

I purchase my coffee—this time it's a different barista, so I don't have to wait as long. I make my way back outside to sit at one of the unoccupied patio tables. Springtime around here can be temperamental at times, so I welcome the pleasant weather and choose to sit in solitude. Lost in the moment, I'm able to purge my thoughts about everything: Dominion House, upcoming graduation, Jaime, and even Cooper.

"Is this seat taken?"

Well, I *was* doing a good job, not thinking about Cooper. Hearing the southern drawl from the other night is enough to snap me back from wherever my mind had wandered.

"Oh, no, go ahead. What are you doing here?" I ignore the inner voices telling me this might be a bad idea and motion for him to sit in the empty chair beside me.

He shoots me a forty-watt smile and heaven help me, my knees begin to knock against each other. I say a silent prayer of thanks that he found me already seated. This way he won't have to witness me fidget underneath the table.

"I was wondering if I'd ever get to talk to you again. I took a chance that this was one of your regular stomping grounds." As he says this, Cooper scoots his seat closer to the table. "Actually, I've been looking for you for awhile now."

Okay, perhaps it's a bit premature on my part to dismiss him right away. He just owned up to looking for me and maybe now he's willing to tell me why. Besides, Jaime's overactive imagination negated any sound advice she might have about potential stalkers.

"Well, here I am." He doesn't have to know that the odds of us meeting up again were pretty low, considering I can't afford to come here as often as I'd like. It's the same as displaying a big neon sign advertising my status as an orphan from Dominion. Today, I just want to forget who I am and enjoy a cup of coffee with a handsome stranger.

"I'm glad." He shoots me another megawatt smile.

"So, do you live around here?" My instincts tell me that even if he answers yes, he's being less than truthful. For some reason, he just doesn't seem like he belongs around here. His accent gives him away for one, and two, there's something about him that makes me feel like he's from a different world all together. But if the voices in my head are correct, then what does he want with me? He doesn't seem the type to hang around a coffee shop chatting up seventeen year olds.

"I rent a room just a couple blocks from here. What about you?" Not taking his eyes off me, he takes a sip of coffee as he waits for me to respond.

"Oh, I live pretty close by." He must know where I live, or he wouldn't have been at Dominion House looking for me, but I'm curious to see how this game of pretend is going to play out. I'm taking a chance that he hadn't been able to get any information about me, so I'm not going to confirm where I actually live. I might be enjoying the attention, but that doesn't mean I have to be totally honest with him. And I'm ashamed to say it, but there's also a small part of me that resents the fact that I live in a home for foster kids.

"Etta!"

I watch as Jaime makes her way over to where Cooper and I are seated. I guess her counseling session ended early. When she didn't find me at the dorm, she must have figured out where I was. Leave it to Jaime to show up just as I'm getting somewhere with Cooper—like finding out why he's been looking for me.

With Jaime here, I'm well aware of how things will turn out and I don't want a repeat performance of the other night. From the look on Jaime's face, I can tell she's steaming and it's going to be bad. Why does she care whether or not I speak to Cooper? But before I even get a chance to apologize to him for whatever's going to happen next, he beats me to the punch.

"Do you trust me?" Cooper reaches over across the table, his hand outstretched. "Let's go somewhere and talk."

Everything is happening so fast I don't have time to register what he's actually saying. And don't get me started on what possesses me to get up from the table, but I do, and allow him to lead the way.

Out of the corner of my eye, I can see Jaime running to catch up, just as Cooper leads me to the side of the building towards the parking lot. He quickly ushers me into the passenger side of a swank white Land Rover. The truck's stark white exterior with black trim reminds me of one of those storm troopers straight out of *Star Wars*.

Claudia Lefeve

I convince myself that what he has to say to me is important. I'm almost eighteen and it's not like I have a secure future after I'm kicked out of Dominion. I have no money, no resources, and certainly no options. There are no provisions for me after I'm legally declared an adult. So I'm taking a chance on Cooper. Maybe there isn't a family that's waiting in the wings to claim me as their own, but I'll be damned if I ignore any opportunities that come my way.

Cooper doesn't say a word as he guns the engine and pulls out of the lot. With everything happening so fast, I don't bother to ask where we're going. Call me stupid, but I decide to follow my instincts. Even though he never got around to telling me why he was looking for me, it's obvious he has his reasons for wanting to find me. No matter how erratic my actions are in response to the situation, I feel like I can trust him.

After a few minutes on the road, I realize we're headed towards the District. "Where are we going?" Even though I still feel relatively safe with him at this point, I still have a right to know where we're headed.

Not answering me, he continues to drive as if he's the only passenger in the vehicle. After what feels like an eternity of silence, he finally turns his head to answer me.

"Somewhere we can talk in private."

What, does he think his SUV is bugged? "This looks pretty private to me Cooper. There's no one in here but you and me," I point out. Now I'm starting to run out of patience. It's one thing to disregard my friend's warnings, but it's quite another to take off with the person she warned you about, only to have him ignore you. I'm slowly beginning to regret my rash decision to join him.

He senses my waning tolerance and pulls the Land Rover off the side of the road. "Look, if you can just hear me out okay? I don't have much time to explain." His face takes on an intense expression. His coal colored eyes twinkle with sincerity. "If you don't like what I have to say, I'll take you right back to the home."

I sit there with my mouth hanging wide open. He knows where I live after all. So much for keeping it a secret. "You know where I live?" I ask, feeling slightly embarrassed. Not because he knows I'm an orphan, but because I now look like a dumbass for trying to cover up the fact when he'd known all along.

"Yeah." He smiles. "And it wasn't easy finding out either, trust me. Took me awhile to figure out where you were."

This isn't the time to get into a discussion about my living arrangements, which is essentially an orphanage, so I let it go. "Okay, talk." I cross my arms to indicate that my patience only runs so far.

"I know you won't believe me, but I have to bring you back."

"Back where?" A small flicker of hope rises in me.

"You know how I just said it wasn't easy tracking you down?"

I nod my head, only because I want to see where he goes with this. This could be what I've been waiting to hear my whole life. I don't want to interrupt him, so I keep nodding to let him know I'm listening.

"Well, that isn't necessarily the truth. I've always been able to keep tabs on your whereabouts. Granted, you move around a lot, but since you always manage to remain in the same general vicinity, it's always been relatively easy to lock down your exact location." Cooper says this so casually, he might as well be telling me he was sorry, but he ran out of gas.

Jaime was right. I was so flattered to have been singled out by him that I didn't stop to notice the red flags. Now here I am, sitting in parked car with a guy I don't even know, who all but admitted he's stalking me. How can I be so dumb? But I'm seventeen for crying out loud. Isn't this the time when I'm supposed to explore new opportunities and talk to hot guys?

"I'm just going to come out and say it." He leans in towards me to make sure he has my full attention. "This isn't your reality Etta. You don't belong here and it's imperative that I take you back home. There, I said it."

"What?" I'm stunned. I don't know what I expected him to say, but this certainly isn't it. I thought for sure he was some kind of attorney coming to tell me I've come into an inheritance or better still, that some relatives in Podunk, Kansas discovered I was stuck here in Virginia. "Just turn back around and take me back to Dominion. I've had enough fun for one day." I glance at the clock on the dash. It isn't even seven yet—I still have plenty of time to get home before curfew.

"This isn't your reality," he says again. "It's not the one you're supposed to be in."

"You're talking alternate realities right?" I now decide it's better to humor him than try to argue. If television taught me anything—and I watch a lot of TV—it's to remain calm when confronted by a crazy person and whatever you do, don't provoke them.

"Sure, alternate realities, parallel universes...it's all the same."

"What?" I ask again. But one look tells me he's totally serious. This conversation has gone from infuriating to beyond delusional at this point. Maybe if I pretend to believe him, he'll tire of this charade and get to what he really wants from me.

Cooper shifts his position in the driver's seat and studies me closely, like he's debating on whether or not to continue. "Like I said before, I don't have much time to explain. Consider whatever you want, but deep down you know on some level that what I'm saying is true."

"Look, if you're into drugs or have some kind of mental thing going on, that's your business. I can hitch my way back home." I rest my hand on the door handle.

"You can make things happen, can't you?" he continues. "With your mind."

My hand slips off the handle, as my body goes slack. How does he know? "What are you talking about?" He may have figured out I'm an orphan, but there is no way I'm going to confirm that I'm a freak too.

"You know exactly what I'm talking about. I know you can make things happen just by thinking them."

"I haven't done anything," I deny, thinking back to all the people I inadvertently hurt just by wishing it. He said earlier that he's always known about me. Does he know about Lester and the others too?

Cooper shrugs. He knows I'm lying. "It's one of the powers you have. It's called psionics."

"Psi what?" I'm beginning to sound like a moron.

"You probably know it better as psychic abilities," Cooper clarifies. "Using your mind to create psychic phenomena."

Claudia Lefeve

I'm so relieved to finally have a name for whatever it is I'm able to do, that I momentarily lose myself in the moment and sit back against the passenger seat. I slowly turn my neck to the side in order to face him better. His eyes make contact with mine and I can see a mutual level of understanding, as if he knows exactly what I'm going to say next.

"Whatever you call it, all I know is, I can make things happen. I can't explain it. Whenever I've felt threatened, I think about making that person stop what they're doing and then..." I can't even finish my thought. Why am I telling him all this? I can feel my face turn red in shame. I don't want to look him in the eye because of the guilt I feel. Even though I was the victim in those situations, it still doesn't excuse the fact that I'm capable of hurting someone.

Cooper reaches out and clasps his hand gently over mine. "It's a form of psychokinesis. Like I said before, you were never meant to be part of this reality. You don't belong here."

"You can't be serious." I quickly pull my hand out of his grasp and inch back closer to the passenger door. "How do you know all this?" This conversation is starting to freak me out. I want to get back to the psychic part of the conversation, not *Science Fiction Theater.* My emotions are all over the place. I want to know what I am, but I'm afraid if I find out, I may not like what I hear. Who the hell is this guy and how does he know all these things about me? I don't know what to believe at this point.

"Stop asking questions for a second and I'll give you the short version. I'll do the best I can to explain."

"Please, by all means." I'm not totally sure I want to hear what he's about to say, but I let my body relax against the warm supple leather, secretly enjoying the feel of the heated seats.

"For reasons I can't get into now, your father brought you here when you were five years old. Over time, he realized this was the safest place for you, since no one had figured out what he'd done. You were safe, so he never saw the need to take you away from this reality," he explains. "But your existence in your real world is paramount. You need to come back at once, darlin'. That's why you have to trust me."

A feeling of numbness washes over me. On one hand, Cooper sounds like a total fruitcake, but on the other hand, there is something about the urgency with which he explains things that make me almost believe him. Almost.

"Sorry, but I'm just not buying what you're selling. How do I know you're telling the truth?" I let him chew on that for a moment. The whole idea of an alternate reality is a little too farfetched—even for a girl like me who does nothing but daydream. And I'm a few months shy of turning eighteen—a little too old for tall tales and bedtime stories.

Cooper sighs. "I don't know what else I can do to convince you. It's your choice. You can either believe me or not."

"Not." It's a risk I can't take.

Claudia Lefeve

Chapter Five
Changing the Timeline

When Cooper was selected by the Council to retrieve Etta from her current reality, he had known it would be a bit of an undertaking on his part. Although he had access to certain details about her—like knowing Etta would eventually come around to trusting him—there was the slightest possibility that she could, at any moment, change the timeline by opting not to go with him. Any decision she made at this juncture in time could split into another reality and he would have no choice but to jump back and start over.

As he listened to himself explain the situation to her, he almost found it as outlandish as she had. He really couldn't blame her for thinking he was some half crazed guy she'd just met—he actually felt like a fool for trying to convince her otherwise. In fact, if their places had been reversed, Cooper knew damn well he wouldn't have believed anyone who tried to feed him the same line he'd just given her. But he didn't have a choice. This was one mission he couldn't afford to fail. And now that he had gotten Etta's attention, he had to bring her back to her rightful world whether she wanted to or not. The decision was simply out of his hands.

It was true when he'd said he'd kept an eye out on her. He had always known where to find her and he could have approached her at any time. True, Etta had moved around a lot as a foster kid, but she always remained in the same city so it never took him long to figure out her location. He simply bid his time until just the right moment to approach her. To Cooper, it was a matter of seizing the right opportunity—selecting a moment in time when she'd be the most receptive towards him.

And having followed Etta's motions the last several years, this had been the opportunity he'd been waiting for. He knew everything about her—what she would or wouldn't do, her weaknesses, strengths, and above all else, her stubbornness. And in all the time he'd spent watching over her, it had pained Cooper to witness firsthand the fortress she had constructed around herself. The hard exterior she had created, coupled with abilities she didn't understand, made her all the more vulnerable. She'd grown up without a proper home and he knew that what she valued most of all was a family. And Cooper felt like a heel because he'd use that knowledge to his advantage.

Chapter Six
I Know What Telekinesis Is

Cooper starts up the engine and faces me one last time before getting back on the road. "I'm sorry Etta, but it's my responsibility to bring you back. This isn't something I signed up for, trust me. What's it going to take to make you believe me?"

I just shrug in response. At this point, there isn't much he can say to add credibility to his story. I can't believe I was dumb enough to get in the car with him in the first place. Jaime is going to be furious when—and if—I make it back to the home. And if I get back after curfew, who knows what kind of trouble I'll be facing.

Just as I'm about to demand, for the second time this evening, that he take me home, Cooper surprises me by saying exactly what I've been waiting so desperately to hear my whole life: "You have a family waiting for you."

Wanting to believe and actually believing are two very different things. But what if even a small part of what he's saying is actually true? If it turns out he's lying, it's not like he can take this ruse very far. What's he going to do, produce a family out of thin air? Doubtful, so I decide to go with it. Perhaps this is his way of saying I have long lost relatives after all.

"Just who are you exactly?" He knows an awful lot about me, but I don't know the first thing about him.

Cooper take his eyes off the road long enough to make sure I'm paying attention. "I'm here to make sure the reality you were taken from reverts back to the way it was supposed to be. We can't change the past, but without you in it, the course of events that are meant to be will be forever altered. It's my job to bring you back to help us make it right."

"Wait a minute. Hold up. If that reality changed when I was taken from it, what happens to this one once I leave?" I can't believe I'm asking him this. I basically conceded the fact that I'm in some alternate dimension.

His attention turns back to the road, but I can see the corner of his lips turn up in a smile. "From the day you made your presence in this world, the timeline changed here as well. Once you go back, everything will revert back to its original course. It will be like you were never here."

The implications of what he just said run through my mind. This means everything I know in this world will change the second I leave it. Everything I touched or came into contact with will be long forgotten. Lester will be alive, continuing to abuse children, while little Maxine will grow up without learning any life lessons. And what happens to Jaime? She'll probably stay at Dominion House without having any knowledge of me. I wonder if she'll have another friend at the home. It was supposed to be us against the world.

And now, thanks to Cooper, I don't even know what world I belong in.

"If it helps, know you are needed back home. You need to trust me on this, darlin'."

"Is that where you're taking me?" Even after all this time daydreaming about it, I never expected it to actually come true. Be careful what you wish for.

"Yes, if you'll let me."

"So why was I dumped here?" What exactly happened to me in this world that I was able to take my counterpart's place?

"Because this is one of the few realities that wouldn't create a paradox—meaning, you could exist here without creating a scenario in which you could meet yourself," he explains. "We can talk more about the mechanics of alternate realities later. Right now, my only interest is to take you back where you belong. Trust me, you are far better off in your real world than you realize."

How much better can that reality possibly be, if it's all messed up without me in it? Isn't that the point?

"Yeah, I guess you're right." It's not like I have to digest everything right away. I won't understand it anyway. "So what do we do now, orb to this alternate world or what?"

The car swerves slightly as Cooper doubles over laughing. "You watch way too much TV. We keep on driving."

"Oh." I don't know why, but I'm disappointed to hear that. "Is that how we get there?" I'm slowly coming to terms with the whole parallel universe theory and I guess I expected to be magically transported to an alternate dimension. I mean, he did mention psychic abilities. "So, you're telling me we can just drive to this place?"

"Yes and yes." He's still laughing. "Yes we get there by driving and yes we're going to magically transport there."

"What do you mean we're going to magically transport? Wait...how did you know I was thinking that? "

"Psionics remember? While you have the ability to move objects, I have the passive power of telepathy. I can read minds."

Holy crap! Exactly how much has Cooper been privy to what's been going on inside my head?

"Will I be able to do that?" I can't believe I just asked him that. Isn't it enough that I can hurt people with the power I already have? Then again, I'm not quite sure I want the ability to read other people's thoughts.

"No. Abilities are either active or passive. And like I mentioned before, you have the active power of psychokinesis," he tells me. "It's also known as telekinesis. That's the ability to move objects with your mind."

"I know what telekinesis is." Even though I'm not an expert on the paranormal, I'm not totally ignorant on the subject—okay, maybe I am just a little. Why did my power always result in someone getting injured? The ability to move objects doesn't exactly equate to hurting people. At least not to my knowledge. So why does it happen around me?

"Your lack of instruction has basically rendered your powers dormant to the point of being useless. I'm actually surprised that you've been able to access your ability here in this reality. But what you said earlier about it manifesting when you feel threatened makes sense. You most likely channel your abilities in fight or flight type situations."

Claudia Lefeve

I consider this tidbit of information. If I'm capable of manipulating objects, which I assume also includes the human body, I'm only somewhat happy to hear I don't have full use of whatever powers Cooper claims I'm capable of. I don't like having the ability to hurt people, even if it is in self defense situations.

As we continue to head north, I look out the window and realize we haven't travelled very far at all. Since leaving the side of the road, I haven't been paying attention to where we're headed. My mind is buzzing over with a million questions, all in different directions, not stopping to fully grasp everything I've just been told, not to mention worrying about where our final destination may be.

The way I understand it, Jaime won't remember me after I leave, but I hope she does. Cooper said this reality will shift back, with everything reverting back to the way it was supposed to be. I guess that that includes memories.

"Look, I know you must have a ton of questions for me, but I promise they'll all be answered soon."

"It would be nice if you didn't rummage around in my head. My thoughts are private." God, I hope he hadn't read my mind that first night we met at Battle Grounds. "And I don't see why you can't answer questions while you drive. I mean, the whole point of all this—I think—is to protect me right? So how am I supposed to feel secure with you keeping things from me?"

"I'm not the one you should be asking, darlin'. You'll find out soon enough. My job is to keep you safe, explain the basics, and bring you back. Everything else will become clear once you return," he said.

"You make it sound like you're taking orders from someone." He said earlier this wasn't something he signed up for. So who's pulling the strings? "Who is it exactly that wants me back? You said something about a father earlier. What about my mom? Is she in this other reality too?"

Cooper's ignoring me again and keeps his eyes on the road. I'm obviously not going to get any more out of him. *Fine, have it your way.*

Pouting like a small child, I slump back into the leather seat. I stare at the clock on the dashboard and realize we couldn't have been driving around for more than fifteen minutes. In fact, we haven't traveled far at all. It's almost as if we've been driving around in circles.

The next thing I know, Cooper announces, "We're here!"

Chapter Seven
The Twilight Zone

Damn! Cooper *had* been driving around in circles. "Did I miss something? How are we here already?" Surely I would have noticed traveling into another dimension. The least he could have done is explain how it worked. He may have weaseled out of answering all my other questions, but this is definitely one conversation I intend to pursue at a later time. But first, I have to figure out where the hell I am.

Since we didn't travel far, I immediately recognize my surroundings. Reading the street signs, I determine that we aren't far from where Dominion House should be. Cooper continues down the street of one of the nicer neighborhoods in Alexandria. Now I know why everything looks so familiar. This is the same neighborhood I lived in during my stint with the Thornberry's. Cooper didn't say so, but I imagine my family must be pretty well off to be able to afford to live in an area like this.

We pull up to the driveway of one of the prettiest homes I've ever seen. It's even nicer than the Thornberry's

—from what I remember. Of course, I spent the last twelve years in foster care, so I don't have a great frame of reference when it comes to real estate, but I think most would agree the house is striking in appearance. The house is a two story colonial, laid with intricate stone masonry. It even has its own gated entrance, guarding a circular driveway. The gate isn't the kind that has an intercom to gain access, but the black cast iron gate is still pretty damn impressive.

Is this where I live? Cooper wasn't kidding when he said my life in this universe is far better than the one I just left behind. Then again, any reality where I'm not foster kid is a big step-up for me.

"Sorry. Jumping realities is another lesson for another time." Cooper kills the engine and climbs out of the Land Rover, while I continue to gawk at the house. "Look, I hate to say this, but you're on your own for now. This is your home and now that you've jumped back, it's like you never left."

As we linger outside, an older looking woman pokes her head out of the front door and waves in my direction. She looks somewhat familiar, but I can't quite place where I've seen her before. Since she seems to know who I am, my fear level goes down a notch. It's still a little nerve wracking to be entering a house you've never been to— that's supposedly your own—but at least the lady appears friendly enough.

"You're on," he announces, as if I'm the star in some kind of Broadway production. "Now that you're back, no one will remember you were ever gone. Unfortunately, you still have the memories of being in the other reality," he

Claudia Lefeve

says, rushing his words. "So you're just going to have to improvise."

Panic sets in. "Wait! You're just going to drop me off here?" For all I know, this is still some colossal joke at my expense. I didn't actually witness our supposed inter-dimensional travel, so I'm not so sure that going inside a strange house is a particularly wise move on my part. Am I just supposed to take his word for it? "You can't be serious." It really isn't a question. But judging his expression tells me he's dead serious.

Cooper gently guides me in the direction of the house. "Trust me, you'll be fine. In fact, you might be surprised how similar this world is to the one you just left."

Sure, except for living in expensive digs with people I don't know.

"Remember, it's your house too."
Quit reading my mind.

He lets out a soft chuckle. "Sorry."

I take a deep breath and take another look at the imposing house before me. I notice the woman has slipped back into the house, but she keeps the front door ajar—I take this as a welcoming sign and take solace in the fact that she knows who I am. Another deep breath fills my lungs as I make my way towards the house. Here goes nothing.

I haven't even taken two steps before Cooper gently tugs on my elbow and draws me close to him. "And try to find out where your father is," he whispers in my ear.

"What..." By the time I twirled around to ask what the hell he's talking about, he's already climbed back into the Rover. I watch in disbelief as he rolls out of the driveway.

Find out where my father is? Isn't he already here in this reality? From the way Cooper was talking, I assumed it was my father calling the shots. Cooper drops me off in some alternate reality under the auspice that my father is here waiting for me. So where the hell is he?

There's no turning back at this point. Apprehension sets back in as I slowly approach the house. The Land Rover is long gone and I don't have a cell phone—not that I have anyone I can call—so I there's no other choice but to enter the enormous house. Maybe the nice looking woman won't call the cops on me when I waltz into her home uninvited.

I loiter in the foyer for a moment or two, while my senses pick up the rich smells emanating from the kitchen. I decide to let my sense of smell lead the way. It seems like a safe bet, considering I don't know the layout of the house. I let my nose navigate like an internal GPS system.

Once I figure out where the kitchen is, I spot the woman chopping up onions on a massive butcher block atop the black granite countertop. She glances up as I enter the room and her smile appears genuine. Catching me off guard, I'm only capable of offering a meek smile in return. It looks like I interrupted her in the middle of preparing dinner. I still can't fathom why she isn't surprised to see me, so I play along. I can't put my finger on it, but I know I recognize her from somewhere.

I'm at a total loss on what to do next, as I watch the lady transfer the chopped onions into a big pot over the stove. In the span of an hour, I've traveled to a different reality, I find out my father is allegedly missing, and I have no idea who this person cooking dinner is.

I've crossed over into the *Twilight Zone.*

Claudia Lefeve

"How was class?" She wipes her hands on the apron she's wearing and moves away from the stove—it smells heavenly, like some kind of stew—and places a steaming pot of hot coffee on the kitchen island in front of me. Not exactly sure what to do, I reach for one of the mugs she'd placed near the pot and help myself. This has to be the teenage equivalent of being served milk and cookies after school.

"Uh, fine, I guess." After pouring myself a cup, I grab a seat at the large wooden table in the middle of the kitchen. Even though the house has a kitchen with modern stainless steel appliances, I can tell whoever designed the place has an affinity for expensive antiques. And by antiques, I mean old. I run my hand over the groves of the old farm wood table and wonder how old the piece actually is. Judging by its age, it must have cost a fortune.

The coffee is beginning to perk my senses, instantly bringing me back to my present surroundings and I carefully observe the woman again, who's gone back to stirring the pot on the stove. She's too old to be my mother and I have no idea as to who she is. It's not like I can ask her. This isn't going to be as easy as Cooper made it out to be.

"So how was your day?" It's the only thing I can ask without giving myself away. Maybe she'll throw me a bone and give me a clue as to who she is. As I wait for her to answer, I wonder what my father does for a living. He's probably a lawyer or some kind of politician. We are in the D.C. area after all.

She adds a few more spices to the pot and turns around to face me. "It was fine, dear. Thank you for asking. Now, who was that handsome young man who brought you home today?"

This time, I'm able to reciprocate with a full smile. She's definitely not my mother. I don't have any experience when it comes to having a mom around, but I had plenty of time observing them as a foster kid. Most moms would grill their daughters about strange men bringing them home after school. But this woman is simply curious. Somehow, it doesn't seem right, not knowing who she is. Cooper could have at least told me who she is before ditching me on her front doorstep.

"That was Cooper. He gave me a ride home." That's a safe answer, right?

"Well that was awfully nice of him. Oh, that reminds me. You should be getting your car back in a couple of days."

"My car?" Perhaps this little reality change isn't such a bad deal after all. So far, I live in a nice house, I have my own car, and the woman looks happy to have me here. Damn, I wish I could ask who she is. Judging from her features, she looks a little like me, so she has to be some kind of relative. Maybe that's why she seems so familiar to me. Then again, brunettes (hers is of the salt and pepper variety) with matching brown eyes is pretty commonplace, so she could be just about anyone. For all I know, she could be the housekeeper.

The woman nods. "I spoke to the mechanic today and they are still waiting for the part to come in. He said something about the part having to come directly from the Mini plant in England."

Awesome. Not only do I have a car, I have a Mini Cooper! Too bad it's in the shop. I only hope I'll get it back

Claudia Lefeve

in time before this whole alternate reality bit plays out. The way things are going, who knows what's going to happen next. But so far, this is shaping up to be an okay world after all.

From the kitchen, I hear the front door open and slam shut. Can it be my dad returning home from work? Cooper must have been mistaken when he said he was missing. I crane my neck as far as it will go for a better view of the hallway. My jaw drops for the second time that afternoon.

"Hey, what happened to you after school? I waited like, half an hour for you."

She has glorious blond platinum hair in this reality too. Cooper didn't say just how much this life here paralleled the one back at Dominion House. Okay, he said it would be similar, but still, what's she doing here? This really is some sort of alternate dimension. Almost like a remake of a bad B movie, starring me in the lead role.

"Jaime!" I want to run up and hug her, but I know this will cast suspicion on me. With her strolling into the house, I imagine this is normal behavior and I'm not supposed to be excited to see her. "Uh, sorry, I got a ride home after school."

She sits down on the nearby stool and studies me with interest. "You could have at least told me you were getting a ride. Just because your car's in the shop doesn't mean you can take advantage of our friendship," she teases.

"Sorry." I don't have to feign feeling bad for having her wait for me. I really do feel bad.

Jaime helps herself to some coffee. "So, who'd you hitch a ride from?"

Still distracted by her presence, I wasn't paying attention to what she just said. "What? Sorry."

"A boy," the woman says. "What did you say his name was? Cooper?" Lucky for me, she answers Jaime's question for me. It saves me the trouble of having to answer her myself. I'm still in shock at seeing my best friend waltz into the kitchen.

"Cooper? Do I know him? He sounds cute. Does he go to Dominion?"

"Dominion?" Like the foster home? Surely we aren't still living at Dominion House in this reality. And if we are, then why we are hanging out in this lady's kitchen? Cooper said I live here, not back at the foster home. Jaime hasn't said more than three sentences and I'm already confused. I guess I better get used to that.

"Yeah, hello? Earth to Etta. That's the place where we spend most of our day reading books and learning absolutely nothing that's going to be of use to us in the real world," she says. "Like calculus."

Reality check: Jaime is still around and we attend a school called Dominion, not Alexandria High. This is turning out to be more like an episode plucked straight out of the *Outer Limits*, not the *Twilight Zone*. Cooper's right; I do watch too much TV. Whenever I was placed in an unfavorable foster home—which was always the case—I was able to escape via syndication. At the time, I enjoyed the weird plots and storylines. Now those storylines serve as a reference point that's beginning to freak me out.

It's pretty clear what I have to do. If I'm going to figure out anything about this new life in this world, I'm going to have to think fast. I need to pry information out of these two without alarming them.

"Yeah, I know, but it reminds me of this weird dream I had last night. I dreamt that I was an orphan and was

Claudia Lefeve

shuffled from foster home to foster home for years. I ended up living at this place called Dominion House for Girls. You were there too Jaime." With any luck, they'd counter the contradictions in my dream.

Jaime snorts. "Thank god I don't have to live in a place like that. It sounds awful. I don't even want to think about what would have happened to me if the Thornberry's hadn't adopted me."

That explains Jaime showing up at the house. Now I'm getting somewhere. She's an orphan in this reality too, only this time around, she's still with the same family that adopted her in the other reality and lives down the street.

"Etta, what a horrible dream. Why would you dream something like that?" The woman comes over and kisses the top of my head. "I'm glad you don't live in a place like that either. Not that there's any reason why you would."

"Yeah, your Aunt Maggie is the best," Jaime says, looking over at the pepper haired woman.

Eureka! So the woman is my aunt. Knowing this pleases me for some reason. I've never been around family before, but if I had, she's the kind of aunt I'd imagine myself having. So that's another mystery down. That just leaves my father. And Cooper's vagueness about my mom is becoming clear. I have a sneaking suspicion she's out of the picture. That's probably why my aunt is here. It's not much information to go on, but it's a start.

Aunt Maggie goes back to the stove and places a lid over the bubbling pot. "Girls, I'm off to get some laundry done before dinner. Don't ruin your appetite drinking all that coffee."

As soon as she leaves the room, Jaime hops off the stool and slides into the chair next to mine at the table. She leans in towards me. "Okay, spill. Who's this Cooper guy and what about Alex?"

Crap. This is an explanation I'm not ready to get into. "No one. Just some guy I know who gave me a ride." Who the hell is Alex?

"Sure," she says, leaning back into the chair. "Don't worry, I won't tell Alex. But I want details girl."

"I swear. There's nothing to tell."

"Uh, huh. Glad you're okay though. I was really worried when you didn't show up after class," she says. "Hey, didn't you just get home? What happened to your uniform?"

Dominion must be a private school. I look over at Jaime and notice her school uniform for the first time. I then look down at my own ensemble of jeans and worn t-shirt. I wonder why Maggie hadn't noticed. "I changed right after I got home."

"Oh. Well, anyways, I gotta get back home. I'm still grounded for breaking curfew last weekend. I just stopped by to check up on you. You know, to make sure you got home okay."

"Thanks for coming over." And I mean it. By Jaime stopping by, I was able to glean what little information I could from the two of them.

While my Aunt Maggie is doing laundry, I take the opportunity and go in search of my bedroom. I climb up the stairs and poke my head in all the different rooms. There are six bedrooms in all. The smaller one has actually been converted into an upstairs office and the last bedroom I peek into can be best described as one occupied by a teenage girl. It's the kind of room I would occupy if I lived in this house, which apparently I do.

I never paid much attention to bedrooms because they were never permanent places for me, but even I have to admit, the room is stunning. I think the style is called country chic, complete with handmade quilts covering the bed and nearby ottoman. The furniture is made of reclaimed wood and the walls are painted a warm olive color with white wainscot paneling covering the bottom half. My body instantly relaxes at the sight. My very own room.

The excitement of today's revelations finally takes its toll on me. All I want to do right now is take a nap. I run my hand over the quilt and crawl into bed. The flowery scents of the crisp cotton sheets beneath me draw me in and I feel a little guilty indulging in the moment. This is someone else's room and I'm an imposter. As much as I want to continue investigating my new surroundings—to prove to myself this isn't just some crazy dream—I can't seem to keep my eyes open.

Chapter Eight
A Ride to School

"Etta, wake up!" I cautiously open one eye and see that it's Jaime, nudging me out of a well deserved sleep. She keeps tugging on my arm. "You have to get ready for school."

"I...what?" I forget where I am for a moment and wonder what Jaime is talking about. I can't seem to shake the dream I was just having. It was different this time—this dream seemed more real than the other ones. I dreamt I'd been taken to another dimension and lived in a beautiful stone house. Even the sweet scent of linens still linger in the air. But it had to have been a dream because Jaime's here, waking me up from it.

"Come on! Get up." Jaime is starting to get annoying. It's way too early to be so demanding.

"Alright, I'm up." I sit up in bed and clean the gunk that's itching the hell out of the corner of my eye.

I glance past Jaime's shoulder and the room suddenly comes into focus. Everything that happened the day before comes flooding back and I realize it isn't a dream. I scowl as Jaime tries to pry me out of bed. I almost ask her to pinch me to make sure all of this is really real. It dawns on me for the first time that I'm now in the company of family and friends and I won't be missed in the other world. There's no one back there to miss me. Everyone that matters is right here.

"Maggie asked me to come wake you up. Now get dressed and let's get some breakfast. You have twenty minutes." Jaime runs out of the room and leaves me to get ready in private.

I don't know which is worse, having my best friend share a room with me, or having her live down the street where she can pop in whenever she feels like it. Mornings are definitely not my most shining hour, especially when I have someone nagging me to wake up.

Considering my upbringing, I've never been much of a clothes horse, so I hope whatever waits for me in the closet is decent. Just because I've taken back this version of myself, doesn't mean I have the same sense of style. But my curiosity will have to wait a few minutes more until after I clean myself up, so I walk past the closet—resisting the urge to open it—and head straight for the shower.

Leave it to me not to notice it before, but my bathroom is *en suite*—I learned that term in school. My very own private bathroom! I do a little jig. I totally take advantage and indulge in a long hot shower. It's nice not having to share a community bathroom or worry about using up all the hot water. I can get used to this kind of life.

After ten glorious minutes, I reluctantly step out of the shower and pad my way back into the bedroom to take a look at the closet. Taking a look inside, I'm disappointed to find row after row of dresses. Nothing fancy, just simple sundresses and one-piece jumpers. I hope this isn't my everyday casual wear aside from school. Venturing further back, I spy a few pairs of jeans, a few dozen t-shirts, and some sweaters. I must have favored a more feminine touch in this world, but for now, I'm happy to don the school uniform I'm required to wear. All that's left is to finger comb my hair and I'm all set.

Using the full-length mirror attached to the closet, I take a long hard look at my reflection staring back at me. The pleated khaki skirt and white polo shirt (complete with the school's crest in the upper left corner), isn't what I picture either, as far as private school uniform go, but at least it's casual.

Jaime raps on the door. "Breakfast? Maggie went crazy again and made enough for an army," she announces, making her way back into the hallway.

Does she spend all her time here? I'm grateful to have her around, but I don't think I can take this type of abuse every morning. I quickly check my appearance one last time before tearing myself away from the mirror. I certainly don't feel like the girl staring back at me in the private school uniform, but I guess this is my life now: new reality, new house, and new clothes.

"Coming," I yell down. I check to make sure I have everything I need. Looking around, I spot a designer looking handbag on the desk. I rummage through its contents: gum, tissue paper, a wallet, and a cell phone—definitely need the latter two, so grab those. I don't see any text books or notebooks lying around, but I manage to find an old backpack hidden behind the mess of dresses in the closet—the fancy purse has to go. The backpack will have to do until I figure out where I kept my school stuff. I shove my wallet and cell into the side compartment and I'm all set.

Sure enough, Maggie is bustling around the kitchen. I detect the scent of waffles. Without turning around, Maggie busies herself in front of the counter, manning the waffles. But she knows when I enter the room. "Well good morning, dear. How did you sleep? You looked so peaceful sleeping last night, I didn't bother to call you down for dinner." She flips the waffle maker over.

There's no excuse for bad manners, even if I did grow up without a proper family. "Good morning. I slept well, thanks. Sorry I missed dinner." And I truly am. I didn't mean to stretch my nap into the early morning. I bet the stew from last night was delicious. I make a mental note to ask about any leftovers when I return home from school.

Maggie just smiles and hands me a plate of waffles. I don't think I've ever seen or smelled anything so yummy. "You two girls eat up," she encourages us, as I graciously accept the food. Sitting beside my plate is a bowl of homemade whipped cream and I greedily help myself to a couple of dollops.

"Blueberry waffles? What's the occasion?" Jaime asks. "Normally it's just regular old pancakes."

"Who cares? They're delicious," I say, stuffing my face. Seriously, this is the best breakfast I've ever had. I wonder if this is a normal morning here at the Fleming household. As I chew, I watch Jaime accept a couple of waffles from my aunt and proceed to drown them in syrup.

"Ugh, so I came over to tell you I can't give you a ride to school today," Jaime says with her mouth half full. "Apparently I broke house rules by staying late after class waiting for you. So mom said she's dropping me off as a way of punishing me." She stops to take another bite of her waffle. "As if being grounded isn't bad enough."

Guilt sinks in again, having Jaime wait up for me at school. And now, getting grounded for it. But I can't help but feel happy for her at the same time. Too bad I can't put things in perspective for her. Here, she has parents who care about her, even if it comes with the occasional punishment. Tough love is still better than being stuck in foster care.

"Sorry," I mumble. "Do we always ride to school together?" Unlike Jaime, I manage to say this without a mouth full of waffles. This is my first meal here and I don't want to look like I don't belong in this nice house. It's important to me that I make a good impression—even if I'm the only one who knows.

Almost as if by magic, the waffles on my plate miraculously disappear. Skipping dinner probably has something to do with it, that and dimension hopping can certainly make a girl hungry. But before I can ask for a second helping, my aunt is one step ahead of me and is already sliding two more waffles onto my plate. She's rewarded with one of my sheepish smiles and I dig in.

"You sure you're okay? You've been acting totally weird since yesterday. Of course we always ride together." Jaime's voice is full of concern. "Your car is way nicer than my Jetta. Besides, I practically live here. Not that my parents ever notice—except when I violate curfew." She winks.

"Since Jaime's mother is giving her a ride, I can run you up to school this morning. Your car should be ready any day now, then you can go back to driving yourselves," Maggie offers.

"Thanks Aunt Maggie." That sounds so weird coming out of my mouth.

Jaime holds her wrist up to check her watch. "Look, I gotta run. Mom is probably pitching a fit as we speak not knowing where I am." Jaime rolls her eyes. "Thanks for the breakfast Maggie," she yells back, heading out of the kitchen.

I scarf the last waffle on my plate and wait as my aunt tidies up before giving me a lift to school. She stops wiping the counters long enough to take a look at me.

"Is everything alright, hon? You have been acting a little confused. Disconnected almost." She walks over to me and puts her hand on my forehead. "Well, it doesn't look like you have a fever, but do me a favor and take it easy today. I don't want you to overdo it in case you're coming down with something."

I study my aunt's face, wondering what side of the family she's from. "Hmm? I'm fine really. Guess I didn't sleep as well as I thought I did."

She gives me the once over as if she knows I'm hiding something. "If you say so," she says, letting me know she's not entirely sure I'm telling the truth. "Are you about ready to go?" My aunt grabs her keys from the kitchen table and wanders out of the kitchen.

I pat my backpack. As ready as I'll ever be.

But we don't get far. As soon as we make our way outside, we notice her car is blocked by Cooper's Land Rover.

Claudia Lefeve

"Looks like you have a ride to school after all." She kisses the top of my head and strolls back into the house. "Don't forget to take it easy today."

I sigh with relief. I'm glad I don't have to go through another round of her second guessing my awkward state on the way to school. That and I'm sure she has better things to do with her morning than to chauffeur me around town.

I immediately run over to the familiar shiny white SUV. "I'll see you after school," I manage to yell over my shoulder before my aunt makes her way back into the house.

"You!" My tone changes the second I enter the Rover. "You have a lot of nerve dropping me off here to figure things out on my own."

Cooper raises his hands in defense and chuckles. "What? No thanks for picking you up?"

"Stuff it Cooper." His amusement at my expense is getting old. He's still sexy hot and all, but a girl can only take so much. "What else have you failed to fill me in on?"

He gently puts the truck in reverse and eases his way out of the driveway. "What would you like to know?"

"My father, for starters. What the hell was up with that cryptic message you whispered to me at the last minute? He's either missing or you just don't know where he is. Which is it?"

His eyes remained glued on the rearview mirror. "You didn't ask your aunt?"

"No. I had a hard enough time trying to figure out who *she* was." I'm definitely pouting. I know it's not a good look for me, but there you have it: I've been reduced to a brat. I realize this is beginning to become a habit whenever I'm around Cooper. He always seems to bring out the spoiled child in me. If he wasn't so hot, I would have stuck my tongue out at him too. "You could have told me."

"Fair enough. But about your dad—honestly, I don't know where to begin. Your dad went missing a few days ago. By the time I finally figured it out, all leads to his disappearance were cold."

"Does this have anything to do with me?" Cooper never came out and explained exactly why I was brought back or who initiated my return. Surely this isn't a coincidence.

Cooper thinks for a second before answering. "I wasn't sure before, but now I'm thinking maybe it does. There are other reasons behind my bringing you back, but I figured that by doing so, it would also undo whatever happened to your dad."

"Kinda like me taking over a life I never left."

"Precisely, darlin'"

"How does this work exactly? Alternate universes, I mean." As he maneuvers his way out of the neighborhood, I can already tell that the one thing that hasn't changed in this reality is the traffic. Rush hour in the metro area can set you behind schedule, even if you're only traveling a couple of miles. So I know we'll be sitting here for awhile. Cooper has plenty of time to explain things while we sit, whether he wants to or not.

"In order to explain alternate realities, you have to think of multiple universes as two sheets of paper lying on top of each other. Now, imagine a small slit that goes through both sheets. If you were walking down the road and slipped through that perforation, you'd now be on the other side of the second sheet. It would be similar, except now you're now on the other sheet of paper."

"Are there more than two alternate universes?"

Claudia Lefeve

I know I'm on to something when I catch Cooper's smile. "Yes. Every time something changes in the timeline, a new reality is created."

"So, instead of two sheets of paper, it's more like a ream."

"Yeah," he chuckles. "I guess you could say that."

"This still doesn't explain how I have parents in this reality, but I'm an orphan in the other."

"Doesn't it? There are realities where you have one, both, or none of your parents. In this scenario, you were placed in another world where your parents died in a plane crash when you were five." Cooper pauses for a second before he continues. "And I'm guessing you died in the crash along with your parents, because like I said before, in order to avoid a paradox, your father must have chosen a reality where you couldn't run into yourself."

It takes a moment to digest this. What he's suggesting hits me: I don't have a mother in this world either. "So here, it was only my mother who died. What changed? I mean, I know I have to expect some differences between the worlds, but why weren't me and my dad on that flight?"

"Because you two were together."

"You mean..." I choke on the words.

"I'm afraid so, darlin'. While your mom was on that flight, you and your father were over in the other reality, making sure you were safe."

I shake my head in disagreement. "Impossible."

"What do you mean?"

I might be new to this alternate reality stuff, but it doesn't take a rocket scientist to figure this one out. "If my father supposedly took me to a place where I couldn't possibly run into myself because I was already dead, how is it that he knew ahead of time? If the events happened simultaneously, how is that possible?" And for that matter, if he knew about the crash ahead of time, how could he allow my mom get on the flight here? The thought leaves me with a sick feeling in the pit of my stomach.

"In all honestly, I can't answer that. I'm pretty limited in what I know. I wish I could tell you more."

Of course he does. "I get it. I have to get answers from my father and he's conveniently missing."

"You know, sarcasm isn't a good look for you. Look, I can't tell you things I don't have the answers to and I know there are things you're finding out that aren't easy to accept, but I'll do the best I can to explain what I do know."

"Fine." I want to change the subject anyway. I don't want to end up being all teary eyed talking about my parents right before going to a new school. *Oh crap, school!* "So tell me about this Dominion Hall Academy then. Why do I go there? It sounds like another institution."

"Well, it should, Dominion Hall is a private school," he says, confirming what I've already figured out. "It's the most exclusive school in Northern Virginia. Actually, in all of Virginia."

"Super." Maybe this universe isn't quite everything Cooper made it out to be.

Chapter Nine
Dominion Hall Academy

There's finally a break in traffic and we roll into the parking lot with several minutes to spare. I sit there, staring out the passenger side window completely stunned. The campus is almost identical to Dominion House for Girls, only the plaque at the front gate reads, DOMINION HALL ACADEMY, EST. 1924. So instead of housing foster delinquents, it's home to the nation's finest youth in the country. The shift in priorities is evident. Even though the sprawling campus hosts the same set of buildings, I'm shocked to see how pristine everything looks. How in the world am I supposed to acclimate myself to this?

Cooper parks the car in front, facing the brick buildings. "I know. It looks the same doesn't it, but different at the same time, huh?"

We stay sitting in the parking lot, staring at the students amble about before class, while I gather enough courage to get out of the SUV. I was able to fool my aunt and possibly even Jaime, but this is an entirely different ballgame. How am I supposed to pretend I've been a part of this world in front of teachers and classmates? They're basically strangers to me. There's no way I'm going to be able to pull this off.

"You're telling me." I cling to my backpack and resign myself to the fact that I'm not in Kansas anymore and suck it up. Hey, school is school, right? How much different can it possibly be it be? At least I know my way around the moss covered buildings.

I know this is a long shot, but I ask anyway, "Are you a student here too?"

"Sorry, darlin'. Been there, done that."

Great, I'm on my own again.

"Ah, come on. It won't be so bad. Besides, you have Jaime. Just stick close to her and you'll be alright."

Easy for you to say.

"You'll be fine, trust me."

"Ugh! Stop doing that!" Cooper's refusal to stop reading my mind infuriates me enough to give me the courage to finally get out of the SUV and face my fears: my first day of school. Not that anyone will know, but on the inside, I'm a ball of nerves. This is way worse than going to a new school for the first time. At least then, we'd all be in the same boat. But here, everyone will assume I know everyone and I don't have the slightest clue as to what I'm doing.

I scramble out of the truck, glad be free of Cooper's intrusion into my thoughts, but stop short, with one leg dangling out the door. "If you're too old for school, just who are you anyway? Or is that something you can't answer either?" I'm being snarky, but he deserves it. "And

Claudia Lefeve

what's up with the accent?" Even though this is Virginia, which is technically the South, you don't hear too many Southern accents this close to the District.

Cooper's face tightens, like he's annoyed, but then lets out a deep laugh. "Boy, nothing gets by you. I may be past my prime, but I'm your friend and I hope you know that. And yes, I can even answer your other question. I'm originally from Richmond."

Okay, being from Richmond explains the slight inflection in his voice and I believe him when he says he's a friend. I don't really have a choice but to trust him at this point. "We'll talk later." I finally manage to extricate myself from the SUV.

Damn, I get several steps away from Cooper's truck and realize I forgot to ask if he's picking me up after school. Oh well, I can figure that out later, I think to myself as I make my way down to the grassy quad in search of Jaime. I assume she's outside waiting for me before class so we can walk together. While I scan the area for her shimmery platinum hair, I feel something hard hit the back of my head.

"Ouch!" I whip around and spot a group of girls playing lacrosse. The back of my head continues to throb where the ball made contact.

"Sooo sorry," a voice calls out followed by hollow laughter.

I'd recognize that apology anywhere. A tall lithe blonde comes rushing in my direction in order to claim her ball. There's no doubt in my mind that she's the one responsible for the pathetic attempt at an apology. Per her usual M.O., she doesn't sound sorry at all.

"Come on Etta, it's not worth getting into it with her." Jaime suddenly appears by my side just in time to grab me by the shoulder. Her attempt is clear: to steer me away from a confrontation. As always, Jaime takes the position of buffer when it comes to me getting into trouble.

Even though I recognized the voice, I still manage to do a double take at the girl running towards us. "Who is that?" I ask anyway, already knowing the answer. I have a feeling this isn't going to be the end of me and Lacrosse Barbie and I want to be sure.

"You sure you're okay? The ball must have hit you harder than I thought. That's Jenny, duh. You know, her dad's the Mexican Ambassador? Access to free booze because her family owns and operates Mexia beer? Super bitch from hell? Ring any bells?" Jaime looks at me curiously. "And judging from bump on your head, she must really have it in for you."

My eyes narrow as I watch Jenny claim her ball and trot back to her group of giggling friends. The Barbie Brigade is just going to have to watch out. If they think they're dealing with the same Etta, they're in for a rude awakening—they have no idea who they're messing with now.

"Why?" It's obvious we hate each other, but I can't imagine having anything to do with a girl like Jenny that she'd actually go to great lengths to make my life miserable. In the other world, it was only logical that she'd be petty enough to make fun of the poor orphan girl. Everyone did. So what reason can she possibly have to bother with me here?

Suddenly, I'm confronted by an affectionate rub on my right shoulder and a male voice. "Hey, are you okay? I saw that ball whack you right upside the head."

I'm mortified that there are witnesses to the most embarrassing moment ever. And on my first day! I subconsciously rub the small bump on the back of my head. "I'm fine, really."

Jaime points in the direction of the male voice behind me. "That's why."

"Oh." I spin around and am startled to be looking straight into the blue eyes of Alex Stewart—the captain of the football team. Wait, does Dominion even have a football team? This strikes me as more of a lacrosse type of school. Why in the world is he talking to me, and more importantly, why in the world does he care whether I'm okay or not? All these questions buzz through my head and it kills me that I can't come right out and ask.

"So, who's the guy that dropped you off?" Alex questions me with a curious look and I can hear the underlying hurt in his voice.

I managed to somehow make the hottest guy in school jealous. Where am I?

"Yeah, Etta." Jaime raises her eyes up at me. "Who's the guy?"

"Just a friend." There, that sounds like safe enough answer. I'm not sure what they know, who they know, and more importantly, what all I'm supposed to know, but it's obvious neither of them have ever met Cooper before. For now, I'll stick to keeping my answers to a minimum, at least until I can get my bearings.

"Well, I'm glad you're okay. Look, I gotta run. Coach has us practicing during first period study hall." He reaches for my hand and squeezes it. "See you at lunch?" He sounds expectant, like there's the slightest possibility I might turn him down.

"Uh, sure." I assure him, not knowing how else to respond. Pleased, he sprints off into the direction of the main building.

Jaime clicks her tongue and smirks. "You don't seem too concerned that Alex saw you with another guy."

"For the record, I'm not with another guy, so there's nothing to be concerned about." I give up trying to explain this to Jaime. And when she mentioned Alex yesterday, I hadn't put the pieces together until now. Is he my boyfriend?

"I think," she begins, linking her arm through mine, as we make our way into the main building, "there's a lot more you're not saying. But don't worry, I'll get it out of you sooner or later."

⚛

Fortunately, taking over someone else's life, even my own, isn't as difficult as I initially thought. Other than not having homework to turn in during calculus class, most of my morning classes go off without a hitch. I just need to make sure to keep my head down and maintain a low profile.

Jaime said she had to turn in some extra credit during lunch, so I have to spend the lunch hour on my own. I avoid my classmates—I don't want to get stuck talking to someone and screw-up royally, so I venture outside and find an empty spot near one of the large oak trees that line the quad. I double check to make sure I'm not sitting on an ant hill and sit down to have a peek at the sack lunch my aunt made for me.

A shadow falls over my paper brown bag lunch. "I thought for sure you'd be sitting with Jaime, plotting something."

I jump, but don't bother to look up. Even though he's only ever spoken a few words to me, I know the voice belongs to Alex. I still can't wrap my mind around the fact that he's standing right here talking to me. Yesterday, I was having lunch at Alexandria High, where he was all over Jenny and didn't even know I was alive. Today he's all about me.

"Like how to get back at Jenny?" Aside from this morning's lacrosse incident, Jenny had also tried—successfully, I might add—to humiliate me in English class when I couldn't recall where we were in our lesson. I'm afraid to look directly at Alex for fear that he'll figure out I'm a fraud.

"Don't let Jenny get you all worked up. She's just jealous." He takes a seat on the patch of grass next to me, but at the same time keeping his distance. Like me, he keeps his focus on the view in front of us.

"Of what?" From what little interaction I had with her, she appears to have it all. Sure, I live in a real house now, with an aunt who cares about me, but not much else has changed. Even in this reality, I pale in comparison to a girl like Jenny. It's not a matter of being bitter, I just can't figure out why her anger is aimed directly at me.

"That's a no brainer. Because I'm interested in you, not her."

Seriously? I hesitate, but I turn to face to him. "Oh, I guess there's that." There's no better way to have the most popular girl hate you than to have the one thing she wants.

"There you are!" Jaime exclaims, coming over to us. She takes hold of my wrists and pulls me up off the ground. "Spanish class is in five minutes, it's time to *vámonos*." She's sounds pleased to be able to use her Spanish vocab words. I don't know what it means—I took French back at Alexandria High but judging by her sense of urgency, I figure it's Spanish for "let's go."

Jaime has horrible timing. She always seems to appear whenever I'm in the middle of talking to a guy. I don't mind being late for class if it means spending an extra couple of minutes alone with Alex.

I take one last look at him before I follow Jaime back towards the main building. "Talk to you later," I say to Alex.

Chapter Ten
The Council

Cooper didn't leave the parking lot until he watched Etta walk into the main building with Jaime. There was a moment when he almost got out of the truck when he'd seen the group of skinny blondes mess with her, but he realized the importance of Etta having to take care of herself and stopped himself. Satisfied she could fend for herself, he slowly made his way out of the lot.

The Council's decision in recruiting Cooper for this operation had been the only logical choice if they wanted to be successful. Their mission depended on her return. When the Council announced Cooper as their pick, he hadn't been surprised, he didn't question it, but he did have reservations about the assignment. But at the same time, he understood their reasoning; he had the most information on Etta and had the best chance of bringing her back home.

It was a long shot, but he knew in his heart it was the only alternative. Still, he didn't like keeping secrets from

Etta, but he was well aware it was for her own safety. Too much information could confuse her and set their mission back. She appeared to be taking everything in stride and he hoped that he could dodge her questions for just a little while longer.

Minutes later, he jumped into his own world. He stared at the dilapidated buildings and smog covered sky. This is what Cooper's home had been reduced to: a grey pit of darkness. His home had once been like any other run-of-the-mill town, devoid of pollution and destruction. There was no doubt in his mind that the events that had transformed this once charming capital city could be changed. One look at the conditions of the town only confirmed his belief that he was doing the right thing.

He stopped staring at the landscape and made his way inside the house. Not wanting to alert his wife to his presence, he had stood there quietly, admiring the way she moved around the room. Her dark brown hair slowly swept past her shoulders as she settled herself down in her chair to review some papers.

Lately, he had found himself feeling guilty about the quality of life they were living. She deserved better than this world and he would be damned if he was going to stand by and let it consume them. That alone was the only reason Cooper had agreed to take this assignment.

Like a voyeur, he continued to watch her movements, as she poured herself into her work. Her position on the Council meant working long hours, with most days spent working well into the night. Neither of them had imagined themselves being part of a rebellion, but here they were.

Feeling his presence in the room, she glanced up from the pile of paperwork, slid off her reading glasses, and smiled up at him.

"Did you see her off on her first day?" She rubbed the bridge of her nose where her glasses had been resting.

He loved it when she did that and smiled at his wife in return. There was no doubt in his mind that she was his soul mate and he couldn't believe how lucky he was to have her in his life. "Yeah, she was nervous as hell, but you know as well as I do, she'll be alright," he said, approaching her.

She rose to meet him and they pulled themselves into a warm embrace, standing longer than necessary, neither of them wanting to let go of each other.

"Do you think we did the right thing? You know, bringing her back?" She whispered.

"You know as well as I do, darlin', it was the only way."

Chapter Eleven
The Old Town Theater

I head straight to the quad to meet Jaime after my last class. For my unofficial first day of school, it wasn't as bad as I'd expected. Maybe I was a bit rash in dismissing private school, but other than my unfortunate encounters with Jenny, it was just like attending any other school—except for maybe cleaner bathrooms.

"So, what do you want to do?" Jaime swings her purse like a pendulum, obviously bored.

"What do you mean? Isn't your mom picking you up after school?"

Jaime rolls her eyes. "Nope. On the way over this morning she said I had to find a ride back home. I guess her parental responsibilities only go so far."

"I don't know. I thought maybe I'd go straight home and see if I could help Aunt Maggie around the house."

"You can do that any ol' time. Let's go to Old Town and check out the scene."

Apparently, she's forgetting the part about being grounded and how her mom busted her the day before for her failure to come home on time.

"What about being grounded?" I don't want her to get in trouble again. I'd hate to see her grounded indefinitely.

"Consider my restriction off. The folks are going out tonight." Jaime's sly smile spells t-r-o-u-b-l-e. "No doubt that's the reason she ditched me this afternoon. She's probably at home as we speak getting all dolled up."

This isn't exactly how I planned to spend the afternoon, but I don't have any other ideas. "I guess we can go for awhile. I'll call Aunt Maggie and see if she can pick us up later." I grabbed my cell phone in such a hurry this morning; I didn't have time to check my contact list. But I have a hunch that I'll find my aunt's number programmed, so I'll just call when we're ready to be picked up.

"Great."

As we walk around Old Town, stopping occasionally to window shop and people watch, I remember Cooper explaining to me that the differences between worlds would be subtle. He wasn't far off in his statement. King Street is still busting with foot traffic and Battle Grounds is still in business, just waiting for patrons to sample their savory drink concoctions. After getting our drink orders, we find an empty table outside.

Over cappuccinos, Jaime begins to reminisce over the fun times we've shared. Slipping an anecdote here and there, sprinkling the conversation with one liners and quotes—things I've said and done—as if she instinctively knows I need to hear this information. It's like listening to a montage of my life. Hearing her speak so fondly of our friendship makes me feel sad in a way. Sad that I don't share the same memories, sad that the girl Jaime recalls never really existed until now, and most of all, sad that my life in this reality has the kind of relationships that I've only ever dreamed about. But all these memories only exist because I came back. They aren't really real—I have to remember that.

I don't want to rehash the good times anymore, so I change the subject. The topic is beginning to spoil the pleasant afternoon Jaime tried to create. There are so many things I want to talk to her about, but I'm sure my questions will only make her think I've gone nuts. Although I have my suspicions that she already thinks I'm nutty. So I stick to a subject that I know Jaime will appreciate—boys.

"So, what do you think about Alex?"

"You know, I'd rather talk about the hunky guy that keeps picking you up. Where is he now? You should call him and have him meet us."

Not a chance. "I don't know. He probably has other things going on." Besides, I don't even know how to contact him. He never gave me a number where I could reach him and I'm certain his number isn't programmed in my cell. "Besides, I already told you. He's just a friend, nothing more."

Jaime points a finger at me. "You are such a liar! There's no way you can only be just friends with a guy that hot."

If only Jaime knew that just a few short days ago, her other self feared he was some kind of stalker. Now here we are, at the same coffee shop, only now she's telling me she thinks he's hot stuff. It's enough to send me to the brink of laughter.

"What's so funny?"

"Nothing." I wave it off. "I was just thinking."

She squints her eyes at me, clearly indicating her skepticism. "You're going to keep him a secret aren't you?"

"Yup." This world is throwing me some curve balls, so I figure I'm owed a little bit of fun.

"Have it your way." She gives up and slumps up against the chair. "But I can't promise I'll back you up when Alex finds out something's going on between you and Hunk."

I know for a fact Jaime will keep any secret I share with her, but now isn't the time. "I'll keep that in mind." Cooper never said I couldn't tell anyone about my switch, but I know that telling my best friend, or even Aunt Maggie for that matter, what's really going on will land me straight into a private room at the local loony bin. For now, I'll keep whatever secrets I have to myself.

We stay a little while longer, enjoying our coffee and it's hard to imagine all the nuances that set these two realities apart. If I sit here and don't think about it, I can almost picture myself back in my other world, sipping coffee with Jaime before heading back to Dominion House before curfew. The coffee in front of me stills sends off an impressive aroma in the air. While the inner nerd lurking inside understands that the term "alternate" implies a variant, my teenage situational awareness can only see as far as what's in front of me.

"Hey, let's go see a movie." Jaime leads the way, tugging at my sleeve as we cross the street, towards the movie theater. The Old Town Theater isn't like a normal multiplex that features tons of movie selections—at least it isn't where I came from. Instead of the normal dozen or so new releases, the theater features only two first run films at

Claudia Lefeve

a time. The place even has a deli and if you're over twenty-one, you can also buy beer.

"I'm not really in the mood to watch—" I start, but the movie posters stop me mid-sentence.

We walk up to the marquee and while I'm pleased to see the theater is still the same in concept, I don't recognize any of the actors, with the exception of Tom Cruise. The Old Town Theater must be some kind of independent movie theater in this reality. Even the titles are foreign to me. None of these films were playing a few days ago: a supernatural flick entitled *Under the Dark Moon* and *Sunset Retirement*, a comedy about old folks.

I wonder if *Twilight* was ever made. Not that I'm a fan of the franchise, but that Taylor Lautner guy, the one that plays the lovelorn werewolf, is totally hot and I'll admit I watched the movies just to watch him shirtless—but only when it got to DVD, I wouldn't have been caught dead watching it in the theater. The vampire, whose name I forget (both the actor and character) does nothing for me. He's way too possessive and wimpy, plus he's too pasty for my taste.

"Did you see any of the *Harry Potter* movies?" I ask Jaime while she's deciding on what movie we should see.

"Harry who? Never even heard of him."

"Really?" This is another series I never read or watched at the movies, but a world without Harry Potter truly means I'm in a whole other dimension.

"Nope."

I have to ask Aunt Maggie where she keeps the DVD player so I can catch up on all the latest movies. Well, actually, more like every movie ever made. I have some major movie watching to make up for. The thought of my favorite movies not existing is too much.

Jaime decides on *Under the Dark Moon*. At least it isn't the Tom Cruise movie. Come to think of it, doesn't his religion believes in aliens? I bet he sold his soul to the head alien in exchange for fame in all alternate realities. He seems like the type.

"You'd think Hollywood would come up with something more original than a movie about werewolves," I say as we pay for our tickets. Paranormal romances are so passé. I can't believe they're just as popular here too.

"Hollywood? Etta, where do you come up with this stuff?"

As Jaime continues to go on about my flakiness, I learn that the state of California doesn't exist anymore either.

After a full afternoon of exploring new my reality, we head back home. Over the phone, Aunt Maggie is only too happy to agree to pick us up after the movie. On the way back, Jaime regales my aunt with stories about my weird observations and behaviors.

"Okay, that's enough fun at my expense." Even though I hate for them to make fun of me, I feel like I truly belong now. It's a nice feeling, being around people that care about me. The only person that's missing from the equation is my dad.

Ultimately, we decide to drop Jaime off at home, rather than have her walk back from our house. This way, she can sneak back before her parent's realize she stayed out late again after school. Aunt Maggie pulls into the driveway of the Thornberry house and snippets of my memory, from the

Claudia Lefeve

time when I lived here as a foster kid, flash before me. The house still looks the same. Actually, it's similar to the one I live in now, but instead of stone masonry, it was laid in red brick with white shutters.

"You better not get in trouble again," I warn Jaime as she gets out of the car. "I'd hate to lose you as friend." If she continues to get grounded, I'll never see her. I should tell her what happens to kids when they threaten public opinion in the Thornberry household. Then again, she's adopted now, not a foster they can easily give back—like they did with me.

"Nah, they aren't back yet. I'm good. I'll call you later."

My aunt waits in the driveway until she's sure Jaime is safe and sound in the house. "I don't envy that girl's parents." Aunt Maggie comments, making her way back to our house.

I giggle in agreement. "I think she just likes the attention."

"I love you both to pieces, but she's a wily one, that girl."

We settle into the kitchen for dinner (leftover stew, yay!) and I finally muster up the courage to ask what I've been itching to ask since my arrival yesterday. "Hey, Aunt Maggie, has dad called?"

"No, hon. I haven't spoken to him since last Tuesday. Why? Is anything wrong?"

Today is Wednesday. That means he's been missing well over a week now. Cooper led me to believe it's been only a few days, but he's right on one count—all evidence pointing to his disappearance is probably long gone. If my aunt hasn't heard from him, I'm at a loss as to whom else to ask. "No. I just haven't heard from him, that's all."

"If he calls, I'll make sure you get a chance to speak with him," Maggie promises.

"Thanks. Look, I'm going to my room for a little while before dinner if that's okay. Let me know if he calls." A few minutes ago, I was sitting in the car laughing and now I can't even bring myself to think about eating. The cappuccino I had earlier is now sloshing around in my stomach, almost to the point of nausea. Maggie just nods and excuses me.

Finding out you're from a whole other world, whose father is missing, with a boyfriend you don't even know—not to mention having a six foot version of Barbie who hates you, is a lot to take in for one day. Struggling with my thoughts, I crawl into bed, but instead of taking a nap, I toss and turn with a million thoughts still rummaging around in my mind.

Lying on my side, I notice a green notebook protruding from the bottom shelf of the nightstand. Reaching down to pick it up, a photo falls from between the pages. It was of me and Alex at some kind of formal. It's kinda freaky looking at a photo of myself with no recollection of having our picture taken or even the event itself. It's like looking at someone who looks exactly like you, only it isn't you, but at the same time is you—just another version.

My fingers flip through the notebook. There doesn't appear to be much written in it. I go to the first page and find a bunch of doodles. The second page contains random phone numbers and to-do lists, which is weird since I'm not a list person. After scanning through the first couple of pages, I notice the notebook has transformed into some kind of journal, almost like a diary. I find it odd that this version of me would suddenly start writing in an otherwise haphazard notebook. I've never been into journaling before, so why would I capture my thoughts in this world?

February 17

I don't know what's been going on with me lately. I've been having all sorts of crazy dreams the last couple of weeks. I read somewhere that having a notebook by your bedside is helpful if you want to jot down your dreams when you wake up. I'm not into the whole diary thing, but I'll give it a shot. Maybe I can go back and read this and figure out what these dreams are supposed to mean.

I'll start with the dream I had last night. I was at home, only it wasn't my house. There was something about it that didn't feel right, like something was off about the whole thing. I'm not even sure whose house I was dreaming about. The scene seemed different, yet so familiar. I know it was only a dream, but it felt so real. Almost like a memory.

The entry is rather vague and doesn't tell me much. What's the point of writing in a journal if you aren't going to jot down any of the details? I guess it doesn't really matter. I didn't exist until the moment Cooper brought me back here. I'm not even entirely sure if anything that occurred prior to my arrival is real. After several more minutes of snooping around in my journal, I put it aside for the time being. It's not like I remember writing any of this. So before my curiosity gets the better of me and read the whole damn thing in one sitting, I decide to take a tour of the house to clear my mind. I'll just make sure to be back before Maggie calls me down for dinner.

Towards the back end of the house, I notice a rather large deck in the backyard through the glass French doors, so I go in that direction and head outside. Quilts, like the ones up in my room, are draped over several lounge chairs, and the stone fireplace off the back end of the deck makes the whole area feel cozy. The temperature has dipped a bit now that it's dark out, so I snuggle up to one of the quilts and soak in the warm heat generated by the fireplace. Aunt Maggie must have gotten it going after we returned home. Yup, spring is definitely my favorite time of year.

"Knock, Knock. I was on my way home and I noticed the back light on. Thought I'd see if you were back here." I hear a voice coming from the back side of the fence.

I almost jump out of my seat. "Damn it! You scared the crap out of me." Where did Alex come from? Does he live in the area too? Probably. All the rich kids live in this neighborhood. I won't be surprised to find out he lives a few houses down from mine, like Jaime.

Alex strolls over to where I'm seated. "Sorry, didn't mean to freak you out. Where's your partner in crime?"

He really is cute. No wonder Jenny hates me. I wasn't expecting Alex to show up unannounced, but I'm glad he did. This gives me a chance to get to know him better. The photo I found in the journal gave me only a brief glimpse into our relationship.

"Who Jaime? She's grounded. Besides, I was a bit tired after we got back from Old Town so we dropped her off. I'm supposed to be taking a nap before dinner." Why am I babbling? He only asked where Jaime was. "What are you doing here?"

"I came by to apologize." He moves the quilt on the matching lounge chair next to mine and takes a seat.

"For what?" Had he done something since lunch?

"You know, for last Saturday. It was all a misunderstanding. Jenny totally busted in on my night out with the guys. I know she told you that it was a date, but you know she's just trying to make you jealous."

"Don't worry about it. I understand." Seriously, Jenny actually did that? Not that I'm surprised, she seems to have the same personality here as she did in the reality I just left. I'm going to have to keep an eye on her from now on. There's no telling what that girl is capable of doing.

"I know you already said it wasn't a big deal, but today at lunch, it felt like you were still kind of mad at me."

He looks so torn, I want to reach out and hug him. It's obvious how much he cares about me. I have to remind myself we aren't talking about a completely different person. We're talking about me. But it's hard to forget that my chances with someone like Alex is pretty much nil to none. Guys like Alex don't waste their time dating girls like me. But here he is and I can have him if I want.

"It's not that. I'm just worried about my dad. I haven't heard from him since he left town for business." I hope my explanation is convincing enough. Anyway, it's the partial truth. I am worried about my dad, I just wasn't really thinking about him when we were sitting under the oak tree during lunch.

"I knew you'd understand. Jenny can be a real bitch," he adds for my benefit. "But you, you're not like that at all. That's why I like you. You seem more determined and sure of yourself."

I hoot with laughter at the idea. "I'm not sure of myself at all. I grew up an orphan remember?"

"Huh?"

Insert foot in mouth, again. "I just mean that with my mother gone and my dad always being away on business, I feel like an orphan." There, that seems like a good save. I'm going to have to make a real effort to watch what I say around people.

"Well, you could have fooled me," he says, accepting my explanation.

Maybe it's the lighting outside—it's already past dusk —or my eyes are just tired, but I can tell Alex is inching his way towards me.

"One thing's for sure. I think you're beautiful." He makes his way closer to me.

"You're just saying that because—" Before I can finish, he leans up against me and kisses me. The kiss is soft, yet purposeful. His hands are cupped behind my head and I can feel him part my lips so he can explore further. It feels like fluttering feathers rippling in my stomach. That's when I stop him.

I've never been kissed like that before. Then again, I've never allowed anyone try to kiss me like that before. In fact, I've never let myself get close enough to anyone in fear that something bad will happen.

"Alex." I push him away from me. "I don't think this is a good idea." As much as I enjoy being this close to him, I can't help but feel a little guilty. Not that Cooper and I have shared a moment or anything, but in the back of my mind, I know there's something that connects us. I'm sure of it. My whole body senses something when I'm around him and I don't get that feeling when I'm with Alex. The kiss was amazing, but until I figure out what it is between me and Cooper, I felt like I owe it to him not to get too involved with Alex just yet.

"Why not?" He looks both stunned and crushed at the same time. "I thought we were starting something good here—I mean, us as a couple," he clarifies.

Now I feel bad about pushing Alex away. He doesn't deserve it. "We do have something, but—I should go back inside." I feel pretty rotten for being a tease, but I can't just sit here and explain why I'm resisting his advances. Single girl survival tip #2: Don't inform someone you just made-out with that you're thinking about another guy.

"No, please don't." Alex slides closer to me. "I just came by to apologize. I don't know what came over me."

"I'm the one who should be apologizing. It's been a long day and I guess I'm just tired." What I want to say is that I do want to be close to him. Here I am, so far removed from everything I know, yet I'm living a life that's supposed to be mine. "Maybe this isn't the best time to talk about this." I suddenly feel sorry for Alex. There's nothing I want more than to keep talking to him, but I know I'm treading in dangerous waters. Someone is going to get hurt.

"I understand. I'll show myself out." He takes his time getting up off the lounge chair. Maybe he hopes I'll change my mind and ask him to stay.

"Thanks for coming over. It means a lot." I must be off my rocker. For years I've had a mad crush on Alex and I'm turning him away for what, another guy who just happens to make my whole body sizzle, who obviously isn't interested in me in return?

"It's okay, we'll talk tomorrow at school." Alex leaves the way he came in, through the side door of the backyard fence.

All of the sudden, I hear my Aunt Maggie through the open French doors. "Is Alex staying for dinner? We have plenty of leftover stew." How long has she been standing there?

"No. Looks like it's just you and me tonight." As soon as the words come out of my mouth, I smile. It's nice to have an aunt to share dinner with.

I rise up from the lounge chair and head back into the house. I pause for a moment to take in the fragrance of the outdoors before retreating inside. Someone had mowed the lawn earlier, I can tell. I can still detect the crisp freshly cut grass. Have I ever stopped to notice things like this before —taking time to stop and smell the roses? I giggle at my own cliché.

"Well, go get washed up. The stew won't sit around forever."

❁

Since I slept in and missed dinner the night before, my first official meal alone with my aunt is a pleasant one. We talk about our day, with me mostly listening to Aunt Maggie talk about her day. Turns out she's a graphic designer and works primarily from home. I think its neat having an aunt who does something cool for a living.

We finish dinner and after Aunt Maggie insists, after much protesting, that she doesn't need help clearing the dishes, I head straight to bed. She still thinks I'm coming down with something and sends me upstairs to rest.

I go to the bathroom to wash my face and brush my teeth. There are so many cleansers and bottles lined up against the vanity that I don't know which one to use, so I wash my face with a regular bar of soap I find hidden in the medicine cabinet.

Claudia Lefeve

And true to her word, Jaime calls right as I tuck myself in for the night. I snuggle up against the sheets and I tell her about Alex's dropping by.

"Seriously? He came over? What did he say?" Of course she wants all the sordid details. "Was he pissed off about Hunk?"

I wish she'd stop referring to Cooper as Hunk. It's getting annoying and every time she says it, I can't help but think about him.

"No, he wasn't mad about Cooper. He wanted to apologize for that incident with Jenny last Saturday. We actually had a good chat." I don't go into detail about the kiss, because I know only too well that Jaime will want to know why I spurned his advances and then I'll have to admit my feelings about Cooper and who he actually is. If it isn't already, my life is beginning to get complicated.

"That's it, isn't it? You're hanging out with Cooper to get back at Alex," she says in a knowing voice. I can picture Jaime sitting up in bed, pointing her long manicured finger in accusation.

"It has nothing to do with Coop. Quit bringing him up." I stifle a yawn. "I'm beat. I'll talk to you tomorrow."

"Yeah, I better get to bed too. I don't want to wake up with those gawd awful circles my mom always ends up getting in the morning. But don't think this conversation is over."

No, I imagine it isn't.

Now that I'm not sleepy anymore, I pull the journal from its hiding place under the bed. I'm not sure know why I hid it, but I'm afraid Maggie might find it. The journal is like a touchstone. Even though it was written by another version of me, just holding it in my hands makes me feel secure. It's a glimpse of the person I would have been had I never left. And if I'm going to learn more about myself, I need all the information I can get my hands on.

March 2

Okay, so I know I'm supposed to be documenting my dreams, but I guess I can write down anything I want. So here goes. Jaime's become a real pain in the ass ever since the Thornberry's adopted her. I know I should feel happy for her, but what gives? You'd think she was adopted by royalty! I've never told her this, but I think Mr. Thornberry is kind of a jerk. I know he's this big deal up in Washington, being the Secretary of Defense and all, but frankly her parents are boring and Mr. Thornberry gives me the creeps. I know I should be more supportive and all. She has a lot of self-esteem issues, but jeez, she's beautiful and whatever. She doesn't need to act all important.

OK, enough about Jaime. Now let's get to the good stuff...Alex spoke to me at lunch today! I really think he's going to ask me out. I can't believe the cutest guy at Dominion might actually be interested in me. After all this time in trying to get him to notice me, I don't know what to do now that he has. I hope he does ask me out. That would make that bitch Jenny super jealous.

Later.

The entry was written only a few weeks ago, so Alex and I didn't date long before I jumped over. In a way, I'm glad we don't have a long history together. This way, I can keep him at arms length until I figure out what to do about Cooper. I like Alex a lot and never in a million years would I ever have imagined him being interested in me and I don't want to hurt him. It's weird knowing that a couple of days ago, I would have jumped at the chance to have Alex notice me. The irony isn't lost on me. But circumstances change and I'm not the same person I was a few days ago. However, if his attention continues to make Barbie jealous, this can actually work to my advantage. It serves her right for treating me like a total loser my first day of class.

I place the journal back in its hiding spot. Instead of counting sheep, I think about all the ways I can get Jenny and the Barbie Brigade back for the lacrosse incident and all the other things she's no doubt subjected me to in the past. It doesn't take long for me to fall asleep.

Chapter Twelve
You Can't Avoid the Inevitable

The next morning I'm jerked out of a deep sleep by the sound of a beep. I slap my hand against the alarm clock, but two seconds later, I hear the beep again. My eyes struggle to open and I notice a flashing light coming from my cell, right where I left it on the edge of the nightstand after my conversation with Jaime. I don't remember setting an alarm on it, so I hesitate to reach out to stop the beeping. Only it won't stop.

Damn. Now I actually have to get up...

I lay motionless in bed, hoping this time the beeping will stop, but there it goes again. Frustrated, I swing my legs over the side of the bed and reach for the phone. Trying to figure out the buttons on the cell, I see another flash of light, and the damn thing beeps again.

"Alright already," I say in frustration.

What I first thought was an alarm, turns out to be a text message. It's a text from Alex.

Want to see you this a.m. Meet me on the back deck before breakfast.

It is way too early in the morning to be texting, so I almost don't respond. I can always pretend I didn't seen the message because I was sleeping. Why in the world does Alex want to meet me before class? We already agreed we'd get together at school. If I respond, I don't want it to appear like I'm encouraging him. What's another hour anyway? In the end, against my better judgment, I message back.

Okay. See you in a bit.

After my hasty text, I take note of the time. It's almost six o'clock in the freaking morning! It's way too early to start getting dressed in my Dominion uniform, so I throw on a pair of jeans and a sweatshirt. I hope Alex doesn't expect me to be all showered and presentable at this hour. Surely I'll have time to get ready for school after he leaves. I don't plan on entertaining him long anyway.

I check myself over in the mirror to make sure I don't have crust in my eyes, when it dawns on me that my current wardrobe has to go. Over breakfast, I'll ask Aunt Maggie if we can go shopping to pick up some new clothes. Wearing outfits from its previous owner gives me the creeps. I know they're mine; clothes that the cosmos picked out for me, but still. In my mind, the girl who chose this wardrobe was an entirely different person.

Satisfied with my appearance, I'm ready to meet Alex in five minutes flat. I'm not exactly sure where he lives and how long it will take him to get here, so I don't want to waste any time. With my cell phone in hand, I rush down the stairs and take a quick peek in the kitchen. Maggie is already there, cooking bacon. Seriously, since my arrival, I've never seen my aunt in any other room in the house. I

Claudia Lefeve

walk back into the hallway. I don't want to get into a discussion about boys and relationships, so I avoid the kitchen. No sense alerting her to the fact that I'm up. I sneak out to the backyard as quietly as I can.

What Alex is expecting to accomplish by coming over this early in the morning, or what I hope to gain from this talk, I don't know. But after what happened last night, I know we can't leave it unsettled. In a way, I'm almost glad he chose to have this conversation before school. For all I know, this could lead to a heated discussion and I'd rather not call attention to myself in the middle of a crowded lunch room.

I'm glad I didn't spend too much time getting ready; Alex doesn't have me wait long for him to arrive. By the time I take a seat in one of the lounge chairs, he's already coming through the back gate.

"Thanks for meeting me." He says with a sheepish grin and takes over the lounge chair next to mine. We're in the exact same spots as we were last night, almost as if we never left.

"Sure. Why so early? Do you think I'm still mad at you?"

"The thought did run through my mind. I just wanted to make sure we were okay and I want to apologize again. This time for being such a jerk. You know, for trying to push you into doing something you aren't comfortable with yet."

I smile to reassure him. "Already forgotten."

Alex clears his throat. "Look Etta, I meant what I said last night. You're different."

"I'm not sure if that's a compliment, but I'll take it. I feel something too, but if it's okay with you, I'd like to take it slow."

"I understand. I came over to let you know that I'm here for you Etta." He moves in closer and takes my hand in his.

"Thanks." I'm flattered he feels that way. Now I'm glad I chose to answer his text this morning.

He leans in and kisses me on the cheek. "I better get back home and get ready for school. See you there?" He gets up from the chair.

"Yeah and I'll even let you walk me to class," I kid.

Alex quietly slips out of the backyard, leaving me to digest everything. I lean back and take in the early morning scenery. Not being a morning person, this is something new. The only thing missing is a cup of coffee. Now I regret not going into the kitchen and grabbing a cup.

All of the sudden, I hear shouting from Alex and a car door slamming. What the hell? I run out the side gate, into the front yard and watch in amazement as Alex is about to get into a confrontation with Cooper.

"What are you doing here?" Alex's chest is all puffed up, ready to take Cooper on.

"Just here to see if Etta needs a ride to school." Cooper, to his credit, takes a step back.

It's obvious he doesn't want to get into a showdown with Alex and I'm glad he backed down. Even though Alex looks like he can hold his own, I know Cooper can take him down quite easily judging by his build.

"If she needs a ride, she can ask me."

Cooper catches me lurking by the side of the house. He looks somewhat embarrassed at having me witness the scene between him and Alex, but recovers quickly. "If it's all the same, why don't we just ask Etta?" Cooper tilts his head in my direction.

Alex's face turns flush when he realizes that I've been standing there, watching the two of them. "Is this the guy who gave you a lift yesterday? What the hell is he doing here?" His eyes suddenly went wide. "Wait a minute. Is this why you turned me away last night? Are you seeing this guy?"

"Yes. Cooper gave me a ride yesterday and no, I'm not going out with him." I hope Alex doesn't notice that I avoided his other question. *Oh yeah, about that. I can't decide which of the two of you I want to be with more.*

Cooper shoots me a confused look. Shit, I forgot he can read my mind.

"How do you even know this guy? Alex demands.

"Just from around." I'm not about to explain Cooper to him. Forget curve balls, the universe is hell bent on striking me out. Why did Alex have to come over and talk to me this morning? Why did I have to answer his text? This scene could have been avoided all together. "Alex, I need to talk to Cooper alone."

"No. Etta wait," Alex pleads. His eyes are brimming with jealousy. "You don't have to talk to him."

I hate to see him so upset, especially since he has no clue as to what's really going on. "I have to Alex. Please, just wait here." I walk over to Cooper and point to the SUV, indicating that we should talk in there.

I look at Cooper and the feelings I had when I first met him come rushing back. His presence alone gives me goose bumps. This is an entirely different feeling than when I'm around Alex. My whole body turns flush whenever I'm around him. My feelings are confirmed when I look straight into Cooper's eyes as we head over to the Rover.

Alex is still behind me. I turn around to face him. "I just need a moment alone with him okay?"

"Etta," Alex says again. "I don't think that's a good idea."

I put my hand up to motion him to stop from coming any closer. "He's my friend okay. He's not going to do anything. Isn't that right Coop?"

Cooper's mouth twitches into a grin at hearing the nickname and he raises both hands up in the air, signaling a truce. "Hey, I'm not here to cause a scene."

"See?" I say turning back to Alex. "We're just going to chat for a second." Satisfied that Alex isn't going to physically stop me, I hop into the Land Rover, remembering to roll the window back up. Cooper must have rolled it down when Alex first approached him. The last thing I need is Alex listening in on our conversation.

Setting my feelings for Cooper aside, I'm going to demand he tell me what he knows about my father. He may stir up some inner emotions I didn't know I had, but he still has information I want to know, so for the time being, I ignore my feelings and determine to be all business.

"So, any word about my dad?"

Cooper stares at me, as if he was drinking me all in. "No. Has he been in contact with you?"

I shake my head in response. "So now what? Why are you here anyway? I still don't know why you keep showing up if you don't have anything new to tell me."

He seems to be more relaxed than he was a few moments ago, now that he's not dealing with Alex. "Chalk it up to curiosity, I suppose."

"You haven't even given me your number so I can call you. How am I supposed to get in touch with you if something happens?" Does he view me as some kind of pet science project? Let's take the poor orphan girl from the foster hell and stick her in another universe. "I suppose you find this amusing."

"No, not at all," he laughs. "There's nothing wrong with me just checking up on you is there? I did bring you here after all. At least allow me the courtesy of making sure you're okay from time to time. And before you say anything else, here is my number." He scribbles something on a scrap of paper. "You may not always be able to reach me, but if you leave a text, I'll get it eventually."

Great, so there's no guarantee I can even reach him if I was ever in trouble. I take the piece of paper and tuck it into my jeans pocket. I glance back up and I can't help but ask, "You're not the one responsible for my father's mysterious disappearance are you?" I probably should have asked that from the beginning. At this point, it seems unlikely that my father is away on business. "You brought me here under the impression that my father was here waiting for me. It's seems a bit sketchy that he goes missing only days before I arrived."

"No, Etta. I don't have anything to do with your father's disappearance. I'm worried about him myself. And I'm not entirely sure why I agreed to bring you back. Maybe this was a mistake on my part."

"I don't understand. You said yourself that my coming back reversed whatever it is that put our reality in danger. Did it work?" I ask.

"To be honest, I don't really know. Did you find anything out from your aunt?"

"I already told you she doesn't know anything. Where do you think he is? I don't even know what he does for a living." Whatever it is, it must be important, judging from the house standing right in front of me. He's probably some sort of big-wig in Washington.

Cooper pauses for a moment. "He's a scientist—an independent contractor for the government."

So he is some sort of government hot-shot. What, if anything, does his job have to do with alternate dimensions? It just doesn't add up. "What part of the government?"

"Department of Defense."

"Oh." Okay, I don't know why I asked as I have no idea if that's good or bad.

Cooper shifts the conversation in a different direction. "So what's up with the guy with the scowl? He seems overly protective of you. Are you involved with him?"

His expression is nothing short of jealous. It's similar to the look Alex had a few moments ago. I don't know what it means, but it pleases me to see Cooper squirm as I mull over my answer.

"What does he have to do with anything?" I let him stew about my relationship with Alex. Besides, I'm getting nowhere with Cooper and this conversation is becoming more and more like a tennis match.

"Just the same, I'd be a lot more comfortable knowing you watched yourself around him." Now, his eyes show a display of concern, but not for my safety. I know he's not saying it because he thinks Alex will harm me in any way. I think it's because he doesn't like seeing me with someone else.

"I'm not doing anything until you tell me why." If I want to pursue something with Alex, it isn't any of Cooper's business. I may find him attractive and he may make my insides tingle, but I don't know anything about Cooper, other than the fact that he can time-travel—and whatever it is he can do. Alex on the other hand is easier to figure out. He's just a seventeen-year-old high school kid whose only major life crises revolve around sports and girls.

"Look, things aren't exactly what they appear to be. That's all I can say right now without altering the timeline. Just know I'm here to look out for you." He starts the engine up. I think that is my cue that this discussion is over. "You better get back to your friend."

I get out of the SUV and watch Cooper roll out of the driveway.

"Just who are you?" I hear myself ponder out loud, watching as he drives away.

Chapter Thirteen
One Feisty Girl

Once he had gotten well away from the Fleming residence, Cooper slammed his fists against the steering wheel. He hated this. Etta had a right to know everything, but he couldn't bring himself to give her the answers she so desperately wanted to know. When he had conspired to bring Etta back, he'd known their mission was the right one, but what he didn't realize at the time was how hard it would be. At least for now, he knew she was safe.

The constant traveling between realities was beginning to wear his body out. While jumps were, for the most part, non-taxing, continuous traveling was slowly beginning to suck the energy out of him.

"That bad, huh? Don't stress yourself out. You said it yourself, this is the only way," his wife said as he entered the house.

He needed to learn how to cover his expressions better, only it was hard to keep his emotions in check around her.

He wiped his shoes on the mat by the door and joined his wife in the living room, where she'd been working all morning. "You're right. I just feel like the biggest jerk, dropping her off in a world she doesn't know."

"If it makes you feel any better, I absolve you of all perceived wrong doings, even if it's for the right reasons," she teased him.

When they had made the drastic decision to alter their reality, Cooper's wife knew her husband would have the toughest job of the two of them. As a high ranking official on the Council, she stood by the Council's decision as a whole, but she could tell the assignment was taking a toll on her husband—both mentally and physically. In many ways, it wasn't fair what she was asking him to do, but they had agreed early on that it was for the betterment of their world.

He laughed. "You're not the one I'm worried about. Etta is one feisty girl." Cooper related the morning's events to his wife.

"Feistier than me? Should I be jealous?"

Cooper had moved in towards his wife and drew her closer to him. He nuzzled her neck and whispered in her ear. "You never have to worry about me, darlin'. I'd travel through all dimensions, hell and back even, to be together with you."

After everything they'd been through, she knew in her heart that what he said was true. "I know."

Chapter Fourteen
Boundaries

With Cooper gone, Alex immediately rushes to my side. He's acting as if I'd been abducted by aliens. Then again, since I'm not entirely sure where Cooper comes from, Alex's apparent concern might be justified.

"Etta! I can't believe you got in the truck with him. What did he want? You two looked awful serious in there." Alex is taking his concern a little bit too far if you ask me.

I can't really blame him. For the last couple of days I'm sure I've been acting totally bizarre and now I have Cooper showing up everywhere I go. "It was nothing, I promise."

He doesn't seem entirely convinced. "Are you sure you're not involved in something I should know about?"

"Nothing is going on. I'm sorry things got a bit out of hand."

"How well do you even know this guy? He could've driven off with you," he scolds me. "How old is he anyway? He doesn't even look like he's in high school."

I assure him that I'm fine and remain unscathed. "Seriously, I'm fine and I promise he's just a friend." I don't know how many times I'm going to have to keep saying this. "If you really have to know, his dad works with mine and I asked him to stop by to see if his dad had heard from him. I've been missing my dad's calls." There. It's as close to the truth as I can get without outright lying to him.

Alex's shoulders drop and he begins to relax. "Jeez, Etta. Why didn't you just say that from the beginning? I was beginning to think you had a stalker!"

I find myself laughing at his comment. Yeah, this wouldn't be the first time someone's thought that of Cooper.

"This isn't funny Etta, what in the world did he say to make you all worked up?" Alex isn't about to let this go.

"He didn't have any new information about my dad, so I was kind of annoyed. That's all." At least this part is true.

I glance at my watch and notice it's time to get ready for school. Alex, instead of going back home, has another idea in mind. He decides to wait until I change into my uniform and offers to give me a ride to Dominion. This is the last thing I need—more questions—but I take him up on his offer, because he isn't giving me any choice. No one told me that dating came with so much drama attached.

After I finish showering, I'm almost ready to meet Alex downstairs when he pokes his head through my bedroom door, just as I'm zipping up my skirt. "You sure you're all right?" He inquires again.

"Hey, privacy!" It's nice having a potential boyfriend, but there are boundaries—and if not, there should be. I'm sure if Maggie knew he was up here she'd escort him right back down to the kitchen where he can sit and wait in front of a pile of blueberry pancakes or something.

Claudia Lefeve

But Alex is undeterred and enters my room once he determines I'm fully dressed. He makes himself comfortable on my bed and I don't bother to stop him. "What's wrong Etta?"

"I think Jaime's on her way. She'll need a ride too," I answer, dodging his question. At least I think she's on her way. Where is she when I need her? She's always around during the most inconvenient times and now she's nowhere to be found. The last thing I need is another moment alone with Alex. I really do like him, but the whole boyfriend thing is all new territory to me. It's bad enough I have to acclimate myself to a whole new life.

"You know Jaime. By the time she finally finishes getting ready, school will already be over," he points out. "So, what did he tell you?"

"You're still with that?" I ask, moving over to the bed. "I already told you, nothing. Look I know I've been acting weird lately, but there's nothing to worry about. Cooper is just keeping an eye out for me while my dad is gone."

"I can do that too, you know. Etta, please. I just want to help. If there's anything I can do, just let me know."

This is clearly an argument I'm not going to win. "Thanks, I'll keep that in mind."

Making sure I'm not going anywhere, Alex slides over to me on the bed, as I inch further away from him. If I shift any more, I'll fall off the bed.

"Why are you being so distant?"

"I'm not. I'm just uncomfortable with you being up here, that's all."

"Do you want me to go?"

I hesitate. "No." I'm taking out my frustration out on him and I know I'm not being fair. "But I guess we should both head downstairs and wait for Jaime."

Instead, Alex moves in even closer and touches my face, tracing his finger along my cheek. "Etta, I don't ever want you to think I don't have feelings for you."

My hand finds its way into his and I lace my fingers through his. "That's what scares me. I'm not...I don't think...I mean I don't know what you expect from all this." My other hand motions to indicate the two of us. I'm fishing and I know it. I want him to tell me if he expects more than just kissing and hand holding. "I need to know what this means to you."

Only he isn't listening. "You are so beautiful, you know that?" Alex gently brushes his hand from my face to the back of my neck and brings it in closer for a kiss.

My body relaxes against his and I let my physical wants take total control. I've never let a guy get this close to me and I'm not sure if I'm ready, but right here, right now, I feel safe in his arms.

He starts off by kissing me gently around my lips, until our mouths meet in a mutual locked frenzy. My body begins to turn hot, then a tingling sensation courses through my body that only worsens as we get closer.

Suddenly, visions of Cooper filter through my mind. This makes me stop as soon I realize where this is going with Alex. It takes all the energy I have to push Alex off me. Here I am, my first experience with a guy—my second, if you count last night—and I'm turning him away. "I can't Alex."

Thinking he's going to be mad, Alex takes me completely by surprise. He stops trying to kiss me and

Claudia Lefeve

looks me straight in the eye. "I understand Etta. Too soon?" He doesn't appear to be angry, but he does look flustered. Maybe he really does have feelings for me that aren't just physical. I imagine that if that's what he's after, he can always get that from Jenny. I'm sure she'd be willing to do whatever he wants.

"I'm sorry. This is all too sudden for me I guess." As I speak the words, I discover I'm not sure if I mean being this close to someone or being in a relationship, but I figure being vague works in my favor until I can figure out which one I have the issue with.

Alex removes himself from the bed. "You're right. Let's go down and see what your aunt's whipped up for breakfast."

By the time we get downstairs, Jaime is waiting for us.

Jaime points to her watch, tapping her foot lightly against the hard wood floor. "What were you two doing up there? We're going to be late for school."

❀

Today, Jaime doesn't have to meet with any of her teachers during lunch. Since the sky is a bit overcast, we decide not to take any chances and eat in the cafeteria. I open my brown bag lunch and find a turkey sandwich, chips, and for dessert, a cupcake—housed in one of those individual plastic cupcake containers. I almost get teary eyed looking at my lunch. It's nice having someone look after me that isn't paid a monthly stipend.

I see a shadow fall across the table. Like yesterday, I assume its Alex, so I look up and smile. It quickly fades.

"So, where's your boyfriend? He ditch you already?" Jenny laughs, her legion of minions stand giggling right behind her.

"Hey, Jenny, eat much?" Jaime points to Jenny's daily ration of diet coke and fruit.

Even though I'm well aware that what she said isn't true —hello, I made-out with Alex in my bedroom this morning for crying out loud—her comment still stings. "Didn't you go out with Alex before he dumped you for me? Oh wait, you never really went out with him. You just follow him around." Maybe the other me stood by and let Jenny walk all over her, but Perky Barbie is talking to this Etta now. This girl isn't afraid to fight back.

"Ladies," Alex addresses the table as he slides over next to me on the bench and smirks in Jenny's direction. He'd clearly overhead the entire conversation.

As Jenny's gaze remains fixated on Alex, I focus on her lunch tray—an apple and diet coke—typical Barbie food—and before I know what's happening, the tray slips out of her grasp and goes sailing past two tables.

Jenny stands there looking completely stunned. "What the hell—"

"Jeez, Jenny, did you trip?" I try to divert the attention back at me and away from her flying lunch tray.

With no witty comeback, Jenny huffs and turns on her heels to go. "Whatever. Let's go girls." The girls quickly fall in line behind Jenny like a formation of birds.

Alex is still laughing at the sight of Jenny storming out of the cafeteria, when I ask, "Please tell me again you were never interested in her. I was talking smack, but please tell me it's true."

Claudia Lefeve

Jaime cuts in before Alex can answer. "Did you really trip her? You just launched her lunch! No one's ever stood up to her before. Poor girl doesn't know who she's up against."

Thankfully, no one was paying attention to how Jenny's lunch tray managed to fly across the room. It's only then I realize that it was my powers that sent her lunch into projectile motion. That's a first. I thought about her tray flying not thinking it actually would. I have to remember to keep my emotions in check.

Alex sits there with a silly grin plastered on his face. "I told you I was never into her. Not my type."

Funny, she was certainly his type back at Alexandria High.

Jaime gets serious for a moment. "I heard about the incident with Cooper this morning...are you sure there's nothing between you two? Do you think you could introduce us?"

News travels fast, I think as I glare at Alex. He's purposely avoiding my stare, knowing full well he was the one who told Jaime about Cooper. I'm sure he figures Jaime will talk some sense into me. Or worse, take Cooper out of the equation—like date him herself. And leave it to Jaime to bring him up right in front of Alex. She knows I'll be forced to deny any sort of involvement. "I guess I could. But I'm not sure if he's already seeing someone. Probably some hot college girl." There's no way I'm going to let her get near Cooper.

She's a little annoyed at the thought of him seeing someone else, but it doesn't get in the way of her trying anyway."Thanks. So hey, when does your dad get back into town? Do you think he'll let you go up to Wintergreen next weekend?"

I've never been to Wintergreen, but I know where it is. The ski resort is just a couple hours south of here, near Charlottesville. I don't know the first thing about skiing, but I think the ski season is already over "I'm not sure. But I guess I can ask Aunt Maggie. Isn't the season over though?"

"Yeah, but my folks still have a cabin. It still gets pretty chilly out at night, so we can hang out in the hot tub."

Alex brightens at the idea of hanging out with me in a hot tub. "I'm up for Wintergreen. Maybe I can ask my mom about your dad's schedule so you can call and ask. She may not know, but she could probably find out," he offers.

"Your mom? Why would she know anything?" Am I missing something here?

He looks confused for a second. "My mom's a senator remember? She might be able to find out if your dad was sent on temporary duty assignment or something. You said you hadn't heard from him in awhile. Maybe there's some satellite that got busted and they called your dad to assess the situation. He's a scientist right?"

Right, a scientist. But I'm momentarily struck by his earlier admission. His mother is a senator? "Yeah, I guess that makes sense. It'd be great if you could ask her. If it wouldn't be too much trouble."

"No problem. I'll ask her tonight." He seems pleased to be able to do something for me.

"Thanks Alex." Looks like I can turn to him for help after all.

"Great. It'll be fun to get out of town for awhile. This place is getting stale," Jaime says, happy we're considering a weekend getaway.

Where in the hell did I end up? My father is some sort of hired gun for the government, probably doing some top secret stuff for the feds and Alex's mom is a United States Senator. Oh, let's not forget a weekend excursion to a ski resort just to use the hot tub.

After lunch, the three of us split up and go our separate ways. I head over to physics class. Even though it was part of my curriculum at Alexandria High, the class here at Dominion Hall is far more advanced. I've been lucky that Miss Stone hasn't called on me but I can already tell she doesn't like me. I don't know why, but every time she turns her attention to me she scowls—which is really a shame because she's actually pretty drop dead gorgeous for a science teacher. I'm sure she'd have all the single male faculty members—the married ones too—drooling over her slim physique and flawless blonde highlighted hair, if only her face didn't always have that pained expression.

It's still a couple minutes before class starts, so I pick a chair and open up my notebook. God, I hope I don't end up failing this class. I wonder if I told Miss Stone that I defied quantum physics and traveled here from another dimension I could get extra credit. I go over how the conversation would play out in my head when I realize someone is talking to me.

"That's a nice backpack you got there Etta. Where'd you score that?" I hear a snicker next to me.

Her timing is remarkable. I have the unfortunate pleasure of being seated next to Jenny—again. Seats aren't assigned in any of our classes, but for some reason, Jenny always manages to seat herself right next to me whenever we share a class. Unfortunately, we're in almost every class together with the exception of Spanish. It's like she waits until the last possible second to take her seat in order to ensure we sit next to each other.

Everyone overhears her snide remark and I quickly shift my legs to shield my book bag. It never occurred to me that my choice in backpacks would be an issue here. I glance over at the floor next to Jenny's feet. Lying beside her is a fancy looking leather tote. I don't know anything about designer bags, but from the looks of it, I can tell it's expensive. My eyes roam along the other desks and spot similar looking handbags and satchels. The school may force us to shield our personalities by having us wear uniforms, but the students at Dominion Hall Academy are still able to express their wealth and personal style with carefully selected accessories.

"I'm not much for flaunting. It's tacky." My face turns red, revealing my embarrassment at having been called out in front of everyone, but my tone remains level. I'm determined not to let her get the best of me.

"Whatever." Jenny dismisses me and opens up her physics book.

This seems to be Jenny's go-to catch phrase, but it sums up the situation quite nicely. I glance back up and notice Miss Stone starting back at me. Once again, her sour expression makes me squirm in my seat.

Chapter Fifteen
Alternate Dimension Travel Agents?

The rest of the afternoon turned out to be pretty boring, or as Jaime so delicately stated earlier, stale. I think I met my drama quota for the day and appreciated the slow paced afternoon. Tonight, I'm looking forward to nothing more than spending a quiet evening at home with Aunt Maggie.

At dinner, Aunt Maggie whips up the most fabulous lasagna from scratch—the pasta is so delicate, you can really savor the oozing mozzarella and Italian spices. It's the best meal I've ever eaten and I'm pleasantly surprised to discover, over idle dinner chat, that I can be myself around my aunt. Not once am I pressured to answer a question I don't have an answer to, nor apologize for my strange behavior. I don't have to lie about what's really going on and I can finally relax. For once, I'm free to enjoy my time here in my new home.

After dinner (this time I'm allowed to help out with the dishes) I do a quick check to make sure my aunt is turned in for the evening and head downstairs. My plan involves a little sneaking around in my father's study. The door to her room is closed, so I take that as a sign that she's already asleep. It's time I play detective and do a bit of investigating on my own. I tiptoe down the stairs and enter my father's study. I'm not sure exactly what I'm looking for, but I guess I'll know it when I see it.

I run my hand along the wall, looking for the light switch and flip it. I know the light won't carry upstairs and alert Aunt Maggie.

"I wondered when you'd finally find yourself in here," my aunt says, scaring the crap out of me in the process.

I jump about ten feet. "Aunt Maggie! What are you doing here?" My aunt is sitting behind the desk, in my father's chair. So much for being stealthy. For a second I wonder if I'm in deep trouble, but instead, she reassures me with smile.

That smile and the way she's looking at me that tips me off that this is something more than just getting caught. "You know."

My aunt nods. "Well, yes and no. I've only just begun to put the pieces together. It wasn't until I came down here that I realized what's been going on."

I take a seat in one of the wingback chairs that face the desk. "So, how did you find out?"

"Yesterday, when you mentioned not talking to your father, I got a bit curious. I then wondered why I myself hadn't heard from him. It's not like him not to call while he's away. So tonight, when I still hadn't heard anything, I finally decided to check his study to see if he left any indication as to where he'd taken off to."

Claudia Lefeve

Excited, I lean closer towards the desk. "Did you find anything?" She must have or we wouldn't be having this conversation. Whatever she discovered, I hope it's something that'll shed some light on my dad's whereabouts and my reason for being brought back here.

She appears to be lost in thought for a moment and then after a second, waves a piece of paper in the air. "Only this letter. It's not much by way of an explanation. And just so you know, I don't approve of any of it, but in the end, I expect his intentions were good."

"What about you Aunt Maggie? Why are you here?" I hope this doesn't come across as being ungrateful. Just the opposite. I'm lucky to have my aunt here and I want her to know that.

She rises from my father's chair and motions me to follow her out of the study. "Come, let's go into the kitchen and I'll explain what the letter says."

Aunt Maggie puts on a pot of coffee and joins me at the old farm wood table. "I came here right before you mother died. My husband, your Uncle Robert, had just passed, and well, my younger brother didn't think it was right, my living all alone. Now mind you, from what I understand reading your father's letter, these are the memories I have now. I don't have any recollection of you not being here," she starts. "But what I know now is that your father sent you away—to a whole other universe no less!" She pauses long enough to take a sip of her coffee. "This is what I found in your father's study." She pulls the letter out of her pocket and hands it over to me.

Dearest Margaret,

If you're reading this, then I'm afraid something has happened to me. In the event of such circumstances, I have made provisions for you and Etta. As you know, darling sister, I have been something of an enigma, even as kids growing up. My fascination in the sciences was something our parents never quite understood. I'm not even sure you did. But you were the best older sister a brother could ever have. You supported me and my experiments and I am forever grateful for this and your own contributions to my cause.

Everything you know in this world is a lie.

I'm afraid I've gone and done something I've come to regret. I cannot go into more detail, as my personal effects could be compromised at any time. But please find it in your heart to forgive me. I only sent Etta away for her safety. If something has in fact happened to me, I can't leave this world without you knowing that all your thoughts and memories of the past twelve years are the result of me and my foolish research. If she is with you now, then she has returned.

Whatever you do, do not contact the police or the federal authorities. To do so will ensure my research will fall under the wrong hands.

If you ever reunite with Etta, please tell my daughter I'm sorry and that I love her very much.

Yours, Victor

Claudia Lefeve

I flip the letter over, hoping there's more to the letter. There isn't. Is this a joke? This note doesn't say anything at all! My father doesn't offer any explanation or information other than what I already know. And everything he says in the letter has all been confirmed by Cooper. I hand the letter back to my aunt.

"From what I remember, I moved here when you were around five. Not only did your father feel responsible for taking me in after Robert passed away, but he insisted I remain here after your mother's passing." My Aunt Maggie says this so quietly, I almost don't hear her. "She had gone to visit friends in Florida and well, you know how that turned out."

I sit without saying a word and I am content to merely listen to my aunt, not wanting to interrupt. I'm afraid that if I do, she'll lose her train of thought.

"That's when dad sent me away." It was only my mother that boarded that flight.

My aunt nods sadly. "You sitting here, right in front of me is proof that you've come back. The moment you arrived, all memories of your absence vanished. It's as if you never left."

She pauses to see if I have anything to say and I shake my head. "Aside from your father, I'm the only family you have. I only agreed to live here so I could help raise you." She gives a weak smile.

At this point I do cut her off. "Wait, hold up. If you are the only other family member I have, where were you when I was an orphan in the world I grew up in? I didn't have to be shipped off to foster home after foster home. I could have stayed with you."

From across the table, my aunt grabs a hold of my hands and squeezes them tightly. "Oh, Etta, I don't know where you father sent you. It could have been one of the many realities where I don't exist. Even if I was alive in that world, I would never have known to find you. But I assure you, it I had known, I would have raised you as my own daughter." Her wrinkled eyes fill with tears. "Make no mistake, I would do anything to be with you."

"You mean you—"

"Know about your father's work? Yes." Her tears dry up and her expression brightens. "I make my living designing graphics for a boutique design firm in D.C., but I also coordinate travels. Monitoring windows, time, and travel conditions. After reading your father's letter, I went back to look at my records. Right around the twelve year mark, the period when your father indicates my memories were altered, I scheduled an opening for him. Only he never told me what the jump was for."

I absorb everything she telling me. It's hard to picture my aunt as a computer geek. She seems so at home in the kitchen, like a thinner version of Paula Deen. But an alternate dimension travel agent? "So you know about traveling to other dimensions?"

"Of course. Your father and I are very close. He told me all about his experiments and travels to the beyond," she explains. "Obviously he didn't tell me everything—I didn't know about you. The second he took you out of this world, was the moment you were lost to me. And here I thought he's just gone on one of his experimental trips."

"Do you schedule trips for other people?" This conversation is getting interesting. It never occurred to me to question Cooper about the possibility of other people traveling to different dimensions.

"Yes, but not many. Travelers are a unique group. Usually they have their own methods or employ trusted individuals for scheduling jumps. You father used me because of my experience and knowledge of computers."

"I'm glad you're around in this world," I suddenly say.

"The feeling is mutual dear." She reaches for my hand across the table.

"That's not all my father did to me is it?" Aunt Maggie hasn't said anything about my powers. I wonder if she even knows. Maybe I'm wrong, but I if my dad could travel to other dimensions, he must also have something to do with my powers.

Theres a flicker of recognition in her eyes. She knows what I'm referring to. I can see it in her face.

"Your father is considered somewhat of a revolutionary. He modernized the scientific field, combining elements of chemistry with physics. Not that many people knew what he was doing, but he developed a serum that can trigger dormant psionic abilities.

"He didn't go into detail about his experiments, mind you, but he often talked about the possibility of our minds reaching its full potential in order to achieve extraordinary powers. As you know, we only use a small percentage of our brains. That's where his research came in. The serum he created was a kind of kick-start, allowing the brain to function to its full capacity."

I let out a whistle. Something like that can be pretty beneficial to the government couldn't it? I now see where he'd be an asset to the Department of Defense. Another thought occurs to me. "I was a guinea pig wasn't I? He used me to test his serum."

"I believe now that he did. When you were little, he claimed he was developing a new type of vaccine booster. Now I realize he was using you as a test subject. His funding didn't allow for human test subjects, so yes, I believe now that he was testing it out on you."

"Are you sure?" If this is true, then I'm not just some girl who randomly has these psychokinetic powers—my father did this to me.

"Like I said before, I wasn't privy to a lot of the experiments your father was involved in. When you were little, I recall him involved in some kind of drug trial...and the participants were children."

"How could he do this to me? And to other children?"

Her eyes moistened up with tears again. "Don't let this information dampen your feelings about your father. He may have been misdirected in his quest for power, but Victor was still a good father. I truly believe he tried to protect you, once he realized his mistakes. That should count for something," she says, trying to convince me to forgive him. "I often wondered if he ever tested his serums on you. But by the time my suspicions grew, you were already gone from this world and I had no memories of you. I had nothing to question him about."

"Yeah, well, now I know why I'm such a freak. I think I've learned enough for one night." I wasn't being rude. I really was tired and everything I had just learned was weighing heavily on my mind. I meant what I said to my aunt—I'm a freak and by my own father's hand.

"You are never a freak in my eyes, but I do agree that you need your rest. We'll talk more about this tomorrow," she offers.

Relieved that my aunt finally knows the truth, I make my way up the stairs to my room. I pull my notebook to read another one of my journal entries. At first, I felt like I was prying into a different person's life, but now, reading my thoughts brings my alternate self closer to me somehow. I begin to view her as an extension of myself, which, for all intents and purposes, she is.

I flip the pages of the notebook until I find the spot where I previously left off.

March 6, 2011

I had another dream last night. This time, I was looking down at myself, like I was watching a movie. I was eight years old and a woman was helping me take a bath. She wasn't Aunt Maggie and I didn't know who she was. It was almost like the bathroom I have here only it was different. The wallpaper was pink with silver stripes. I don't know why, but it felt more like a memory than a dream. The woman reminded me of my mother. I miss her so much.

I woke up pretty disoriented and cold. It was like I had actually gone somewhere that took all the energy out of me. I hope I don't have another dream like that again. They say that waking up soaking wet is a sign of night terrors. But it was more like a cold sweat and they definitely weren't nightmares, I'd remember. I just felt even more tired after waking up.

On the home front, things are finally settling down between me and Jaime. She's spoiled, but in truth, I love her. She's my best friend after all and I shouldn't write bad things about her. It must be tough to be in her shoes, being an orphan and all. Always being insecure and wanting to be the center of attention. I guess I can't really blame her for simply being herself, even if she is selfish and spoiled.

'Til next time!

The notebook almost drops out of my hands. I re-read the first couple of paragraphs. I was describing the bathroom in one of the foster homes I had grown up in. I remember the house with the pink wallpaper with silvery stripes. How in the world did I have memories of me over there? Is it possible that I actually saw myself in that reality, even if it was only in my dream?

Claudia Lefeve

Chapter Sixteen
Pool Party

After last night's revelations, I only end up getting about four hours sleep, so needless to say, I'm a bit of a wreck when Jaime shows up to pick me up for school. I still haven't heard back from the Mini dealership, so I have to rely on Jaime for a ride, now that she has her driving privileges back. Her parents finally gave in and she's no longer grounded. I'm in the middle of picking at the eggs benedict Maggie has prepared for me.

"You look like hell," Jaime says, helping herself to breakfast.

Now I know why Aunt Maggie spends so much time in the kitchen—she has the unofficial responsibility of feeding all the neighborhood kids.

"Gee, thanks." I sop up the remaining hollandaise sauce with the last piece of my English muffin and pop it in my mouth.

"Seriously, what'd you do? Stay up all night? And why wasn't I invited?" Jaime pours so much hollandaise on her plate you can't even see the rest of the dish. It's absolutely gluttonous. I wonder how she manages to stay so thin.

I should really take a cue from my own journal and give her a break. She is a little spoiled, but I know she has my back in any fight. I peek over at my aunt. "I guess you could say I stayed up. I didn't sleep very well last night."

"Right and I'm sure the visitor you had yesterday morning doesn't have anything to do with it. Tall dark and handsome can do that to a girl. Don't forget you promised to introduce us."

I made no such promise, but I let it slide. "No, it's not that. I just stayed up late watching TV when I couldn't fall asleep."

"Yeah, sure."

Aunt Maggie nurses her coffee and shoots me a wink, allowing my little white lie. It's nice being able to share my secret with someone that isn't Cooper. My aunt may not have all the answers, but I know I can count on her to help me figure things out as they come.

My feelings are so mixed, I'm not sure who knows what at this point and what other secrets are possibly being kept from me. I know I can trust Jaime, but I'm not sure if I'm ready to disclose what's really going on with me. So for now, I want to keep my conversation with my aunt close to the vest.

"Etta, I almost forgot to tell you. While you were upstairs getting dressed, I got a call from the dealership. Your car is ready," my aunt informs me. "If we hurry, we can go pick it up before school, then you can drive yourself."

"Awesome." Jaime sounds more excited than I do. "I'm going with. I love riding around in your car."

Yes! Finally, I'll be able to roam around town without having to rely on anyone. I clear my plate in the sink and meet my aunt at the front door with Jaime trailing right behind me.

The Mini dealership is only minutes away from the house and I'm so stoked to be picking up my car, you'd think I'm being presented with it for the first time. Then I remember this is the first time I'd be behind the wheel of my very own car and I get excited all over again.

My aunt accompanies me over to the reception desk. I sign the appropriate paperwork as she pays the bill. Then all three of us wait outside as they bring my car around the front of the building. As soon as I lay eyes on it, I instinctively know I had picked the car out myself. The dark green Mini convertible is exactly the kind of car I would have chosen. I run my hand along the slick shiny hood and wonder for the millionth time how I ended up in this world.

Aunt Maggie understands why I'm so excited and whispers in my ear, "Have fun."

Once I'm behind the wheel and Jaime's safely tucked behind the seatbelt, I tear out of the dealership in the direction of Dominion Hall. While I don't have much experience driving, I had taken the mandatory driving course at my old high school. At the time, I was a bit resentful being in a driver's ed class where most of the students would be getting their own car when they turned sixteen. Now I'm grateful for the instruction. I have no problems whizzing in and out of rush hour traffic in my little Mini.

"Jeez, Etta. You act like this is the first time you've ever driven," Jaime says, shaking her head. "Dial it down a notch or you're going to get us killed before we even get to school."

"Sorry." I let up on the gas. "Just glad to have my car back."

"Ditto, but take it easy will ya?"

The drive to school was entirely too short, but I can't waste time driving around. We have to get to class or we'll get in trouble for being late. I can always take the long way home after school. I didn't hear from Alex this morning, but I manage to spot him before heading off to first period.

"Hey, I tried calling you last night." He rushes up to meet us in the quad.

I feel a bit guilty as he runs up to us. Before I decided to ransack my father's study last night, he called and I allowed it to go straight to voicemail. "Sorry I didn't call back. I was charging my phone and I didn't hear it ring," I say. "I probably wouldn't have heard it anyway, I had a bad dream and ended up sleeping in the living room."

"What was it about? I hope I wasn't the cause of the nightmare," Alex jokes.

And an opportunity presents itself. "Actually, we were both in public school and you were the quarterback of the football team." Offering Alex a dose of the truth, albeit veiled as a dream, is just what I needed. It's cathartic in a way. I'm getting tired of all this secrecy bull crap.

"That doesn't sound so bad, but I'm captain of the lacrosse team."

"Yeah, I know." I don't, but I do now. "Oh, but that's not all. I was also a foster kid and you wanted nothing to do with me. In fact, Jenny was your girlfriend." I wait for his reaction.

Alex hoots with laughter. "You're right. It does sound like a nightmare."

"It was so real," I go on, continuing to milk it for all it's worth. "I can't seem to shake that memory from my head." It's kinda fun teasing Alex, but at the same time, it's nice to be able to tell him the truth, even though he thinks it's only a dream. That and it's also payback for not keeping the other world Jenny in check.

Jaime joins us after saying goodbye to a girl I don't recognize. "What was real?" She'd missed half the conversation.

"Oh nothing, Etta's telling me about some bizarre dream she had where I was dating Jenny."

"Sounds more like a nightmare," Jaime shudders.

"That's what I said," Alex agrees. "So tell me more about this dream. Did you have a boyfriend?"

"No. But I had a major crush on you though." I decide to throw him a bone. I owe Alex that much after the way I've treated him the last couple of days.

"Really?" He weaves his arm through mine, obviously liking what he hears.

"Well, duh, who wouldn't crush on the captain of the football team? Too bad you were with Jenny. She was a real major bitch, kinda like the way she is now and you were all over her," I tease.

Alex pulls away and puts his hands up in mock defense. "Okay, enough," he laughs. "I think I'm going to have my own nightmare tonight."

"Was I in your dream too?" Jaime asks.

Clearly she didn't like to be left out. "Yeah, the Thornberry's never adopted you because Mrs. Thornberry had a little problem with business ethics."

Jaime rolls her eyes at me. "That dream again? What did you call the place we lived in? Dominion House? Can you imagine having to live in a place like that?"

Yeah, I can. It's proving more difficult not being able to confide in the both of them. Everything they've ever known is merely a life that ends up getting duplicated in another reality—every time a choice is made, we end up playing out a different scene—like a choose your own adventure book.

"Nope," I say instead.

"Etta was up watching movies all night. Don't let the bags under her eyes scare you," Jaime giggles.

"Oh, hey, I want to see if you have plans tonight. It's Friday," he points out.

"All three of us?" I really don't want to be alone with Alex tonight. I can totally see myself going out with him, but I'm still a little hesitant. So for the time being, if I can drag Jaime into doing whatever he has in mind, I'll feel a lot better.

"Uh, yeah, sure. Jaime, you game for doing something?" He sounds disappointed, but extends the offer anyway. I can tell he had no intentions of asking her to join us, but I'm part of a package deal—at least for now.

Even while planning a somewhat date with Alex, Cooper's perfect bright smile still lingers in the back of my mind. I haven't heard from him since yesterday morning's showdown with Alex. The slip of paper he gave me with his phone number is still tucked in my jean's pocket back at home. I promise myself that if I don't hear from him this evening, I'll call him myself. Single girl survival tip #3: It's never a good idea to call a guy first. Not that I'm an expert on the matter, but desperate times call for desperate measures.

"She's in. What's the plan?" I take the liberty of agreeing for the both of us.

"I thought since the weather turned out pretty decent today, maybe we could grill out over at my place after school."

"Awesome," Jaime squeals with delight. "I love your pool Alex. We can have ourselves a mini pool party."

"Awesome," I echo back. I guess his initial plans for an intimate date has turned into a party. Do I even own a bathing suit? I must. I just hope it's not a revealing bikini.

There are some things that never change, no matter what reality you're in. Like springtime in Virginia—it can be cold and unforgiving. But today is unusually warm and the idea of going over to Alex's house after school is appealing. I've never been friends with someone who has a pool. Suddenly, I begin to look forward to my quasi-date with Alex.

When I arrive at Alex's house after school, I'm totally taken by surprise. It's amazing what a difference a street makes. And I thought my own block was impressive. Cherry blossoms and grandiose oak trees line the street, showcasing colossal two story colonial homes, with the Stewart property boasting the largest plot. Who knew being a public servant paid so well.

I'm glad Jaime and I took the time to help Alex set-up the backyard. The cook-out we planned earlier this morning didn't turn out to be exactly the small affair we'd expected.

Word quickly spread about Alex's little get-together and soon his entire backyard begins to fill with kids not only from Dominion, but all the neighboring public high schools, including Alexandria High. I even spot Amy Pierce, sporting a red striped bikini. I guess she doesn't get knocked-up in this reality. At least, I hope she's not pregnant; she's on her third bottle of beer.

"Hey, Etta."

I'm perched along the pool's ledge, dangling my legs in the cool water and I momentarily push aside the noise gathering from the crowd. I can faintly hear someone calling my name from a distance. After a few more calls for my attention, I finally look up to find Jenny scowling down at me.

"Spaz much Etta? Don't think for a second I don't know it was you. Your little Frisbee stunt in the cafeteria isn't going to scare me off. Can't figure out how you managed to get that close to me, but you better watch your back," Jenny warns me. Her face is so scrunched up; she looks like she just swallowed a sour grape.

I did my best not to laugh right in her face. Now that I know I can defend myself, I'm not so scared of Jenny anymore. "I'll keep that in mind."

Jenny and the Barbie Brigade venture off to the other side of the pool, where lounge chairs are arranged along the pool's edge. I continue to watch Jenny as she applies sun screen to her fair skin and decide I can't help myself. I focus my attention on where she's sitting and pretty soon, the whole group watches in shocked amusement as Jenny's chair buckles under her, propelling her directly into the pool.

"Holy crap, Etta, did you see that?" Jaime races over to me, where I continue to soak my legs, just as Jenny's head bobs back up.

"Front row seats." I giggle, taking in the full view of Jenny as she splashes around in the water. Too bad I can't take the credit. I mean, I'm totally responsible for causing her chair to break, but I can't admit it.

"You've got guts laughing at someone like Jenny," she laughs alongside me. "What's gotten into you? It's like you're becoming this whole other Etta." She takes a closer look at me. "I like it."

From a distance, I watch Alex grin as he endures Jenny's wrath. Despite my earlier misgivings, I'm beginning to warm up to the idea of being his girlfriend. What he lacked in humor before, he certainly has command of it in this world. A guy who can laugh at the small stuff can't be all that bad. So what if I don't get the body tremors around him, like I do when I'm with Cooper.

"God damn it Alex! Can't you afford better chairs? My hair is soaking wet!" Jenny wails at him for a full five minutes. I'm pretty sure she's going to call the evening short. "I can't believe I brought over free beer for you guys."

She pads along the tile floor, making her way back towards my direction. "And you," she hisses. "You just better watch it." With the Barbie Brigade right behind her, they quickly make their escape. Everyone continues to laugh as her wet feet almost cause her to slip on the tile flooring.

"Don't slip," I sing as they walk past me. It's a childish thing to say, I know, but she had it coming.

I'm late getting back home from the party, but I read another entry in my journal before bed. I could've read it all in one sitting when I initially found it—it's not that thick of a notebook—but for some reason I want to pace myself. Savor what little connection I have to the life I was meant to have led.

March 10

He finally asked me out! I can't believe it! Can this really be happening? Now I just hope I have his attention long enough for him to ask me to the Spring Fling. The girls at Dominion will just freak if they see me with Alex! I can't wait!

So that's where the photo was taken. Guess they—we—went to the Spring Fling after all. It's weird reading about your life, never actually experienced it yourself. I wonder if there is anyone else in the world that's gone through this. Then I remember the promise I made to myself earlier to contact Cooper. I still haven't heard from him, so I dial the number that was written on the scratch sheet of paper. The phone rings several times and goes straight to voicemail. I hate leaving voicemails, so I start over and send him a text.

Hey, where are you?

Hopefully it won't take long for him to respond back.

Chapter Seventeen
Travelers

The next morning I find myself being lulled back to sleep to the gentle sound of rain. The taps against the window form a random rhythmic pattern that doesn't sound random at all. I'm still a bit groggy from the night before (Jaime and I got stuck helping Alex clean up the backyard after the pool party which is why I got home late) and my body is totally regretting it.

For once, since having returned, I don't have anything scheduled, so I go in search of Aunt Maggie. The first place I check is the kitchen and she's not there—that's a surprise. I head back upstairs and locate her in the converted bedroom I noticed on my first day here. This must be her office. I peek through the open doorway and observe my aunt hunched over the computer monitor working on some kind of computer program I don't recognize.

Sensing my presence, she turns around in time to catch me studying her. I'm not spying, just keenly interested in what she's doing. Who knew my aunt was up to date on all this computer stuff? Most adults I come in contact with are still trying to figure out PayPal and online banking. And here she is, effortlessly designing graphics, not to mention coordinating travel jumps in her spare time. I'm suddenly struck with a sense of pride towards my aunt.

"Etta." She greets me and motions for me to join her at the desk. "Do you want to see something?"

"Sure." I pull up one of the side chairs by the desk and sit next to her, getting a full view of the computer screen.

"Would you like to see how I arrange travels?"

"You can do that? Show me, I mean?" This goes way beyond cool. My aunt seems pretty open minded about sharing information about the whole traveling to other dimensions. Which is more than I can say for Cooper. He didn't even text me back last night.

She exits out of her current program and quickly opens up another one. "Here, let me show you a hypothetical jump." In a few short key strokes she's constructed a chart. "Let's pick a date in the future to plan our make-believe jump."

"How about my birthday?"

"Perfect! May twenty-fifth." Aunt Maggie doesn't even bother to see if she got the date right (because she was) and begins to type in the date. Aside from my birth date, she also enters the following day, May twenty-sixth.

I can't believe she's really going to show me how all this works and tell her so. "I can't believe you're showing me this."

"Nonsense. Why wouldn't I? Your father introduced you to this world; you ought to at least know how it works." Aunt Maggie shakes her head as she hacks away at the keyboard. "Sometimes I wonder about my brother."

"That's pretty cool." I watch as a pentagram begins to take shape on the screen.

"Now, see the dates at the bottom of the pentagram?" She asks, making sure I'm paying attention. "Good. These are our going to be our travel dates. The subsequent dates on the other points of the pentagram are the returns, with the top point representing your constant, see?"

I nod my head again to show I understand.

"Okay, now take a look at the lines." She makes a trail with her finger along the computer screen. "These represent our destination jumps. Each corresponds with arrival and departure jumps."

I'm surprised to find it's really rather simple once she explains it. I could probably come up with a similar chart using Word or something. "That's it?"

Aunt Maggie shoots me a knowing smile. "Of course not. That's the easy part."

That figures. "If there are only two dates, why are there five points for each jump?" Each of the two lines had five separate points, with lines connecting them together, similar to the main pentagon frame.

"Those are the available open windows for each of those days," she explains. "Travelers may end up at a different location from where they originally jumped and need another window to access the portal back. The points you see are the variable windows."

"So what if they need to stay longer or something happens that prevents them from leaving on their designated day?"

"Each traveler is assigned their own device to make changes for departures and in some cases, arrivals."

That's why Cooper was so insistent on bringing me back that day. He already had a scheduled opening for us to jump to this reality. "Okay, so now that you have the dates and stuff, what's left?"

"It's all plugged into a system. Once everything is configured, it goes through a process of probabilities and sequences to determine optimum windows," she goes on. "I'm afraid that part is a little more complicated, but I can show you if you'd like."

"That's okay, I get the idea. So who are these traveler people?"

Aunt Maggie studies me, debating on whether or not to continue. "Travelers are a very select group of individuals that were specifically trained to jump between realities."

"How does my dad fit into all this?"

She sighs. "He studied and acquired the technology to travel between parallel universes."

And he used that knowledge to transport me to a different reality. "So why do you think I was brought back to this reality after all this time?"

Aunt Maggie looks thoughtful for a moment. "I wish I could answer that for you, but I don't even know why your father sent you away in the first place. If he had bothered to confide in me, I'd be better equipped to help you figure things out."

"I think my being here may have something to do with dad's disappearance."

"It's quite possible, dear," she says. "I just wish I knew more."

"Do you think we're doing the right thing? I mean, by not calling the cops?"

Claudia Lefeve

My aunt gives a frustrated sigh. "I'd like to think I know your father well and if he says not to contact them, then I guess we have to respect that. He has his reasons."

"Okay, we won't call them."

Knowing I'm not going to get any more answers on the subject, I steer the conversation back to a topic my aunt does know something about. "Can anyone go through these portals? I mean, what if someone is walking along, minding their own business, and happens to pass through one of those?"

"Highly unlikely. Do you know who Stephen Hawking is dear?"

I may stand a good chance of failing physics this year, but I know who the genius physicist is. "Yeah, he's the guy in the wheelchair."

"Good. Well, he theorizes that billions of parallel universes are connected by wormholes—don't worry, I'm not going to go into a lesson on wave functions," she says noting my expression. "Basically, the premise is simple: of all the universes, ours is the most likely, but certainly not the only one."

"How does that answer my question?"

"Well, if each parallel universe is connected by a wormhole, or portal if you will, the actual connection is extremely small. However, there are opportunities for larger windows to allow passage. That's where the program I showed you comes in to play. So while it is improbable for someone to find themselves at the other end of an alternate universe, travelers are able to pass through successfully."

"So what you're saying is that it's rare for someone to fall through one of those wormholes unless they know about it," I say.

"You catch on fast, dear." She kisses the top of my head. "Now, how about some breakfast?"

Chapter Eighteen
Painted Ladies

Sunday is the only day of the week that actually makes me believe there's some sort of distortion in the space time continuum. You can always count on weekdays to follow a normal time pattern, Saturday seems to run on forever, but on Sunday, the hours are set on warp speed. One minute, you're enjoying Sunday brunch, then bam, you're suddenly cursing your alarm clock on Monday morning, ready to start the week all over again.

I'm in a sullen mood by the time I wake up—no surprises there. Cooper didn't respond to my text until earlier this morning. Once again I was awakened by the beeping of my cell when his text came through. I have to figure out how to silence the damn thing before I go to bed at night. I had plans to veg out in front of the TV all day, but apparently Cooper has another idea in mind.

I'll be over later this morning. Wear something comfortable.

I text back wondering what's so important he has to see me in the morning, not to mention the comfortable clothing.

What are we doing?

Going back to the basics. It's training day.

Okay. What time?

Let's shoot for 11a.m.

So after I inform Aunt Maggie that Cooper is coming over after breakfast, I wolf down a massive plate of pancakes—I'm so going to gain about twenty pounds by the end of the month if she keeps feeding me like this—and head outside to meet Cooper for what he's dubbed 'training day'. I have no idea what this means, but I liken it to something out of the *Karate Kid*. Not the new one with Will Smith's son, but the Ralph Macchio version. Although I'm sure the analogy would probably be lost on anyone else. I don't think that movie was made in this reality either.

Cooper shows up a couple minutes early and waits for me out back on the deck. "A beautiful day to train, don't you think?"

"That depends. What kind of training are we doing? And why are we outside?" I can't imagine my training has anything to do with exercise. I'm a total couch potato and if he thinks we'll start the day by running ten miles, he's sadly mistaken.

He straightens up. "Nature is still the cornerstone of our abilities. Our powers rest on the balance of all things living," he explains. "That is why you are able to control a person's actions with your thoughts. We have the power to control the body as well as natural elements."

"You never told me how you ended up with telepathic powers. Hey—were you one of my dad's test subjects?" It would be too coincidental if he wasn't. The only logical

156
Claudia Lefeve

explanation is that we both were subjected to the drug trials.

"Ah, another story for another day," he says mysteriously. "So you found out about that huh."

I don't see any reason why I can't, so I tell him about my conversation with Aunt Maggie. "Yeah, my aunt told me. She knows by the way."

"I guess your aunt would know about your father's research."

"I'm kinda glad she knows, you know? Now I don't have to keep secrets from her. It's not like you're always around to talk to anyway."

"Touché."

"So we're out here for what exactly?" I ask.

"Well, you've already proven that you can make the human body do things by wishing them to happen—"

My mind flashes back to Lester. *Yeah, and I ended up killing a man.* Then I remember that by me leaving, everything reverted back to the way things were before I arrived in that reality. I realize he's no longer six feet under. But I imagine it's only a matter of time before he'll be paying for his sins.

"I'm going to pretend I didn't hear that," Cooper says. "But since you brought it up, I think you've mastered the art of manipulating the human mind. Now you just have to focus on living things that aren't persuaded or governed by thought."

Embarrassed that he read my thoughts again, I can feel my face turn warm. I think I know where he's going with this. "Like plants and trees."

"Exactly. People can be easily influenced when we use our powers, but it's much harder to control living vegetation, animals, and insects. Even though you'd think they would be the easiest to control, it's actually much harder. They're living, but they don't have minds to bend."

"What about the incident with Jenny's lunch tray? And the pool chair?" After seeing his puzzled expression, I explain the encounters I had with Jenny. Those weren't living breathing things, they were inanimate objects.

"Really? You did that? I'm impressed," he chuckles. "Objects, much like people, are the easiest to manipulate. Think of it this way, objects are created by humans to be used by humans, therefore objects are the easiest of things to control."

"How do you know all this stuff?" Cooper talks like he could give a presentation on telekinesis to the local psychic women's group.

"Oh no, today is about you," he says, bringing us back to the topic at hand.

I'm beginning to regret contacting Cooper. He's so frustrating! Now I'm certain he's keeping things from me on purpose. If the circumstances had been different, I wonder if my dad would have shown me how to use my powers. At this point, anything is better than having Cooper teach me.

"I'm sure he would have." He sounds hurt upon hearing my thoughts.

Stop reading my thoughts.

"Sorry. Your mind is wide open right now," he points out. "To be honest, it's not often I can read your thoughts. You usually keep yourself pretty guarded."

I think about that for a moment and shrug. "When you come from a world where you're shuffled around from family to family, and some of them not very nice, you kind of have to."

"Good point."

"Okay, so now that I know why we're out here, what is it you expect me to do exactly?"

"We're going to work on your psychokinetic skills. The little stunt at lunch and at the pool shows you have the power to manipulate inanimate objects, so we are going to strengthen that power. Seems to me you came upon it fairly easy, channeling your frustration towards Jenny to make those objects move, but now we're going to get you to move things by utilizing control versus emotions," he explains. "You're going to dance."

"Excuse me? You don't call for days and you expect me to dance with you?" He has a lot of nerve, coming over after days of not hearing from him.

"What, too soon?" Cooper teases. "Besides, I'm not offering. You are going to choreograph a rather difficult, but most magnificent dance. You're going to call upon the Painted Ladies."

"Who?" Why am I even amazed anymore? Fine. If Cooper says I'm going to dance with some old ladies, then so be it.

"You should spend more time in your garden," he chides in a mock tone. "Painted Ladies are butterflies."

I snort. "You expect me to gather a bunch of butterflies? I'd have an easier time catching bees with my body covered in honey."

He eyes me up and down with a wicked grin. "Unless that's an invitation for me to smear your body with honey, I'd stay clear of comments like that. I'm likely to take you up on it."

"I'll keep that in mind." I muffle a giggle. As soon as the visual pops in my head, I quickly dismiss it. I'll just bet

Cooper is poking around in my head trying to figure out what I'm thinking. "So how do you expect me to get these butterflies to come to me? I don't even see any around."

"You know what your problem is?"

"I didn't make time to eat my Wheaties?"

"Funny, but no. You lack confidence, darlin'."

Hey! I have plenty of self-confidence. Is it my imagination or did I not stand up to Jenny and her merry band of the Future Trophy Wives of America at the pool party? My confidence might be lacking in areas, but only when it comes to guys.

"I think you're being overly dramatic," I say to Cooper. "And my name's Etta, not darling."

"We're going to work together on this. I'm going to call them and you're going to make them dance."

"Why are we doing this anyway?"

"Because you need to learn how to use your abilities. You were right, what you said before. I'm not always going to be around and if your father's disappearance is any indication, you might be next, darlin'. And the only defense you have is your power."

Cooper has a point. If someone does find out I'm back, I could be in some serious trouble. At the very least I can learn to control my powers better so I don't accidentally hurt anyone. "Okay then, shall we dance?"

"I'd thought you'd never ask." He smiled.

Cooper centers himself in the middle of the backyard and closes his eyes. After a few minutes, I tire of waiting—nothing's happening. He continues to stand there motionless, like he's in some other place, almost Zen-like. I can tell he's concentrating, but I don't see any butterflies coming toward us. This is a complete waste of time. It's

Claudia Lefeve

probably too early in the spring for butterflies to be out and about.

Then I feel something flutter against my arm—a butterfly. Several more glide by and hover around Cooper. He opens his eyes, while his body remains fixed in the center of the yard. "Now that I've called them here, I want you to make them dance."

"Coop, I have no idea how to do this." What does he expect me to do? I don't know how my power works. Sure, I can make Jenny's life a living hell, but I can't just make butterflies perform at will. Can I?

I watch the butterflies crowd around Cooper, there has to be at least thirty of them now—how the hell did he do that? I close my eyes and think of a spiral. My mind stays focused on the image. I open up my right eye and peek to see what they're doing. Nothing. They're still fluttering around Cooper. I quickly shut my eye back up and think of the spiral I have created in my head. Cooper's not saying anything, so I know whatever it is I'm doing isn't working.

"It's not enough to visualize it. You have to force it to happen."

Ya think? "Ralph Macchio had it easy. He only had to learn that stupid crane move," I mutter under my breath.

"What was that?"

"Nothing. Just thinking out loud."

I rid myself of every thought that's going through my head and I picture the spiral once more. This time, I don't just imagine it; I actually make it turn in my mind. My body goes rigid as I continue to focus. *Turn.* The spiral rotates up with no immediate end—an infinite swirling corkscrew. It feels like I'm really rotating it, like a spin-top. *Just turn.*

"Etta," Cooper whispers in awe.

Oblivious to everything around me I hear, "How magnificent!" and "You did it!" all at once. I open my eyes and discover a giant swirl of Painted Ladies spiraling around Cooper, just as Maggie rushes behind me and grabs hold of my shoulders.

"What in the world," Maggie exhales in my ear. "Etta, did you do this?"

I momentarily lose focus and when I turn to address my aunt, the butterflies flutter away.

Cooper waits until the last Painted Lady exits the backyard and strolls over to us. "Not bad for a newbie, huh?"

"It was enchanting," Aunt Maggie breathes. "Did you show Etta how to do this?"

"Only the basics ma'am. It was all Etta."

"You must be Etta's friend Cooper," my aunt reaches out to shake his hand. "I've heard so much about you."

"Have you now?" He shoots me a wink.

"Oh, please." Why is Aunt Maggie toying with me? The only time I mentioned Coop is when he dropped me off that first day and this morning, when I told her we were going to hang out. When I explained to her that he was the one who brought me back, she was so grateful that she said he was welcome anytime.

"Well, I'll leave you both to get back to work," my aunt says as she gently guides me along with her towards the house. She shepherds me over to the front of the deck. Obviously she has something to say that she doesn't want Cooper to overhear.

"What's up?"

"I like him and I'm happy he's helping you dear. Learn from him," she says out of Cooper's earshot. "I have a feeling you're going to need him more than you realize."

I shoot her a quizzing look.

"I'm an old woman. Trust me on this. I know these things," she says with a knowing smile. "Call it an old wise woman's intuition."

She pats me on the shoulder as she makes her way back into the house. It's just me and Cooper again. I can't help myself and run straight into his arms. "I did it!" I squeal.

Cooper wraps his arms around me, in what I assume is a mutual victory hug. We hug for several moments, neither of us wanting to let go of the moment.

"Hope I'm not interrupting anything. Although the visual of you two doesn't leave much to the imagination," a voice calls out from behind us.

I pull myself away from Coop's arms and whirl around to see Alex coming from inside the house. "Alex! I didn't know you were here." Aunt Maggie needs to start imposing rules regarding visitors. How much had he seen?

"Your aunt Maggie let me in," he says as he retreats back into the house. "Right, well, I guess I see where I stand."

"No, Alex wait!"

But it's too late.

Cooper is amused by the exchange and stands back quietly as Alex storms off before he turns his attention back to me. He has a smug look on his face, like he's pleased about what just happened. Do I detect a hint of victory?

"So what's really going on between you two?" He finally asks. "He'll get over it by the way. If you want, I can tell you exactly what he was really thinking."

"He's kinda my boyfriend, ya know." Wow, that sounds weird coming out. That's the first time I've said that out loud. "I thought I was supposed to play along? You know, messing up the timeline and all. You're the one that said that any changes could be detrimental to this reality." I'm purposely goading him and he knows it. There's no way I'm telling him that my feelings for him are getting in the way of any relationship I hope to have with Alex.

"Aw, it's already too late for that Etta, darlin'. If you want to go out with Alex, don't let me stand in the way. But you don't have to, you know," he drawls. "Besides, my main concern is you at the moment."

"I still don't understand why." Isn't that the million dollar question?

"Because I may be the only one who knows the way it's supposed to be. You're the one, Etta," he says.

I stare at him blankly. "The one what Cooper?"

"Let's just say you are a remarkable young woman. One I'd like to see stay alive long enough to take over her true destiny."

"Fine. Just so you know, I'll date who I want, when I want, but don't get any ideas about the two of us exchanging more than just training exercises. You got that?" He may draw out emotions in me I don't understand, but I can't allow myself to succumb to them. What would be the point?

He moves in closer. "Are you sure you're not a little bit attracted? You're sure giving off mixed signals."

Tingles go up my spine. Is my body language giving off signals? Am I that obvious?

"Aren't you full of yourself," I say, calling his bluff.

"Your eyes give you away." He leans in even closer.

Don't get too excited. He's just messing with your head. "Whatever."

Cooper is now dangerously near, close enough for me to smell him. The same scent of licorice and cloves. "I promise you, my intentions are completely honorable."

Don't fall for it. "I don't believe you."

He then does the unthinkable, or rather, something I thought would never happen. He grabs me by the arms, binding our bodies together as one. His lips seek out mine in a passionate frenzy. My tongue parts his lips, wanting to fully savor him and I lose control of the situation. Then just as suddenly, Cooper breaks away from our embrace and breathes in heavily. "There. Our deal is sealed with a kiss," he says triumphantly.

The kiss momentarily catches me off guard. I can't think of what to do or say, so I slap him. "Don't even think you get to do that to me again." Okay, I know I'm just as guilty; I wanted it too, even more if that's possible, but my mind is still fuzzy over what just happened. What am I doing? This whole time I've been pining for Cooper and I go and slap him. But I continue my tirade, "You're welcome here for the sole purpose of helping me figure all this out, but that's it. Our time will be limited to training. I don't want to see you otherwise."

Cooper retreats back, respecting my space. "Duly noted," he says with a smile and a twinkle in his eye.

Chapter Nineteen
Beyond the Call of Duty

Cooper couldn't get out of the backyard fast enough. He had waited until he was safely in the Land Rover before he pulled himself back together. He didn't want to let Etta know just how shook up he was over what had just happened.

"What the hell was I thinking back there?" He muttered to himself in disbelief.

He had almost blown it, kissing Etta like that, but he couldn't help himself. True, it had been an exciting moment, for both of them, watching her work her magic on those butterflies, but it was still no excuse for taking advantage of the situation. She had looked so happy and vulnerable at the same time, he couldn't resist. But as much as he had enjoyed the moment—minus the slap—he knew he was going to have to tell his wife about the exchange.

What Cooper actually felt worse about was his frustration over Etta's relationship with Alex. She was vague about her situation with the kid, but he had a feeling she was doing that on purpose. He was a seventeen-year-old kid for and at twenty-two, he should know better than to be envious.

His instinct to protect Etta bordered on overdrive and he would do anything in his power to keep her safe. Even if it meant crushing the dreams of a high school senior. His need to watch over her went well beyond the orders handed down from the Council. No one had ever said this was going to be easy.

He arrived at the old abandoned industrial complex, situated right outside the city limits. Because of its rundown appearance, it ensured privacy from the military forces that patrolled the inner capital city. The complex had been appropriated years before by the Council to use as their mission support center. Cooper knew he would find his wife there. He only hoped she would understand.

"You're back early," she said, noting his return. "I'd thought you guys would be training all day."

"Yeah, well...things ended pretty quickly after I, uh, got slapped," Cooper said.

It took her a moment, but then her eyes shone with the realization of what he was admitting. "Cooper, you didn't!"

"Darlin', I'm sorry. It just happened," he said. This was a conversation he never thought he'd have with his wife, but he was glad he came clean. Confession is good for the soul, he thought.

To her credit, his wife didn't appear overly upset by his admission. Slowly, she rose from her chair at her desk and looked into her husband's eyes. "Maybe so, but let's just hope this doesn't ruin things," she said. "Something like this could totally confuse her and we need her on board."

Claudia Lefeve

Chapter Twenty
Spring Fling

After the incident with Alex, I decide to give him a call to make amends. I offer up some sorry excuse why Cooper was over and Alex accepts my lame apology. He's more forgiving than I originally gave him credit for and more forgiving than I actually deserve. I even manage to smooth things over even further by inviting him and Jaime over for Sunday dinner. No one turns away a dinner prepared by my Aunt Maggie—even if her niece is a major jerk.

Of course, it thrills her to no end to have a full house for dinner. She prepares linguini with clam sauce and I swear it's now my favorite meal. Perhaps I overestimated my apology to Alex earlier. He, along with everyone else at the table, eats in silence. I can tell my aunt is disappointed because everyone's just picking at their food. Alex is throwing doubtful glances at me due to this morning's incident. And I don't even know why Jaime is so silent. Maybe she thinks I don't deserve Alex. Who knows?

Alex clears the tension with an announcement. "Uh, my mom is having a fundraiser Tuesday night. I was kind of hoping you could come."

"Really?" This catches me off guard. Maybe he's not mad at me anymore. "As in a date? What kind of a fundraiser?" I immediately picture boring old politicians wearing suits and eating off of cocktail napkins. It doesn't sound like my idea of a fun date, but after what happened this morning, I'm willing to do anything Alex suggests—well, not anything.

"It's actually a black tie kind of event."

Scratch business suits and make it appetizers and tuxes. There's no way I'm going to get out of going and besides, I owe him one. "Sure. I'd love to go." After all, it isn't everyday you get invited to a party hosted by a senator. Come to think of it, I might just get a chance to ask his mom about my dad. Alex did mention they knew each other.

Alex beams. "Great! I'll call you with the details tonight when I get home."

It's as if the slow motion button switches to real time. Now that Alex and I have officially "made up", everyone, including Jaime, stops fiddling with their meal and digs into the amazing linguini. I'm not even going to imagine how things would have played out if he'd actually shown up a minute later and witnessed the kiss Cooper and I shared.

My excitement is genuine, however, from the outside, it looks like I'm happy to be going to his mom's fundraiser, but on the inside I know it's for all the wrong reasons. I fully intend to use this event to my advantage—get Alex's mom alone to ask questions.

Claudia Lefeve

Maggie begins to clear the table after everyone excuses themselves for the evening.

"There are some formal gowns in your closet," she says as I hand her empty plates.

"Thanks."

"We can always go shopping if you'd like. I know it can't be easy wearing clothes that someone else picked out."

"No thanks. I'd rather go pick up some more jeans if that's okay with you. There's really no point in spending money on a dress I'll probably only wear once.

"Of course." She hugs me, plates and all. "We'll make some time next weekend."

"Aunt Maggie?"

"Yes dear?"

"One of these days you're going to have to put a lock on the front door."

My aunt chuckles. "Yes, I suppose one of these days I will."

⚛

March 19

Tonight's the Spring Fling. Alex was so sweet when he asked me to go. He even looked excited about going. And I'm finally going to meet his mom for the first time. I know dad isn't too thrilled with me dating, but he'll get over it.

I don't know why he always gets nervous whenever I bring up Alex. Guess he's afraid I'm all grown-up now. He probably doesn't know how to handle a dating teenager. Thank god I have Aunt Maggie. She is the only one who can talk sense into dad. She even helped me pick out a dress. It's the cutest grey taffeta dress.

What a letdown. No dreams in this entry. I pull the photo out from where I tucked it in the back of the journal. I take a closer look at the couple. I'm not a fan of dresses, but it's definitely cute.

I head straight for the closet and find the grey dress. It's a simple poof dress with a halter style top. Only it isn't grey like they way it's described in the journal, it's more shimmery platinum. *My dream!* This is the same knee-length formal I dreamt about when I was at Dominion House. How is this possible?

I re-examine the photo that's still in my hand and try to picture the meeting between the other Etta and Alex's mom that night for the first time. Any mother would have been impressed to have their son date a girl like the one smiling back at me from the photo. Even though we're the same person, I don't think I could have pulled off looking as good as the girl in the picture. There's a special look in her eyes. All those years being in foster care robbed me of that.

My thoughts are disrupted by my cell ringing. I bet it's Alex. I look at the number on the screen. Yup, it's Alex. I can't not answer it, especially since I just smoothed things over between us. "Hey," I put on my sweet voice. "I was just thinking about you." I'm still staring at the photo of the two of us, not taking my eyes off their smiling faces.

He doesn't say anything, but I hear him breathing on the other end of the line. I wait patiently until he finally says, "Are you sure? Not that Cooper guy?"

"Just you. Actually, I'm looking at the photo we took at the Spring Fling."

"One of these days you're going to have to tell me about him." Alex ignores my last comment.

Okay, I deserve that. "You don't need to worry about him."

"You're right, I won't. Besides, you're going out with me on Tuesday, right? You haven't changed your mind or anything have you?"

"Not in the last half-hour. I'm actually looking forward to it." But not for the reason you think.

"Don't sound too excited."

Am I that transparent? "Seriously, I'm really looking forward to going. Are you sure your mom won't mind me hanging around her party with all those political types?"

"No way, she knows I hate these things. Anything to make her only son happy."

Maybe her hospitality will extend to answering questions about my dad. If my dad works for the government, there's a small chance Senator Stewart would know what he's up to.

We say our goodbyes and promise to meet up in the morning for school. Not ready to fall asleep just yet, I go back to Etta's journal.

March 20

The Spring Fling was a total bust. And worst of all, I don't know what I did. Alex was so excited to introduce me to his mom and everything was going really well I thought, until right before we left for the dance. His mom got all abrupt and it's like she couldn't wait for us to leave. Later that night, Alex was acting all distant and didn't seem like he was very happy to be there. Did his mom not like me? Did she tell Alex something?

Then, Jaime gets all drunk and I had to call us a taxi to get her drunken ass home. Alex didn't want her to puke in his truck, so I got stuck paying for a taxi to get us back. Some fairy tale dance. And to top it all off, today, Alison tells me during tennis that Jenny was all over Alex after I left the dance. What a bitch.

What happened that night that made his mom did a one-eighty? And what was up with Alex being a total jerk? I keep on reading.

March 26

What the hell? Jenny is going out with Alex now? Jaime just called and told me they were seen at the movies.

March 28

I'm not even going to write about Jenny and Alex. I'm done with them. Alex tried to talk to me at school, but I just ignored him. I don't really care what he has to say.

But I did have another dream last night. This one is weirder than the others. I was at Battle Grounds and I meet the most gorgeous guy. Then Jaime makes me go back to some dorm room where we lived. The dream seemed to fast forward and the next thing I know, I'm driving around town with him.

Why can't I meet someone like that here? I bet he wouldn't go out with someone like Jenny. Oops, wasn't going to mention her.

That was several days ago! Her—my—dreams are almost in sync with my reality. How is this possible? I flip to the next page. Blank. This was the last entry written. I check the date. This was two days before I showed up here. And the entry about Alex, what's up with that? He ditches me for Jenny, and then apologizes to me in the backyard, saying that it's all a misunderstanding? This is a timeline that's played out as if I truly always existed in this world.

Chapter Twenty-One
$1,000 a Plate Dinner

Alex doesn't pick me up or show up at the house with flowers. Nothing to suggest that this is supposed to a typical date. Instead, he calls to tell me he has to help his mom set up for the event and wants to know if I can possibly come over on my own. So, I head over to Alex's house all by myself, which is fine. His place isn't that far from my own, so I decide to walk. I don't know how many people the senator is expecting, so I'd rather not go through the trouble of finding a parking space that's just as far as my own house.

I walk up to the Stewart house and for some reason, I'm not as impressed as when I first went over to his house for the pool party. The absence of moonlight just made the neighborhood look, well, dark and uninviting. I continue up the drive and notice that the senator arranged valet parking for this shin-dig—guess I didn't have to worry about parking after all.

When Alex first told me his mother was a senator, I was a bit confused. The way I understand it, most members of Congress hole themselves up in tiny townhomes in the District while in session, while their families live in much larger homes within their home state. So, I did a Google search on Constance Stewart and it turns out she's actually a senator from this district, so it only stands to reason that this is where she keeps her primary residence. The Wikipedia page on her didn't mention a husband, so I assume Mr. Stewart is out of the picture.

Alex must have ESP—which by now wouldn't surprise me if he does—because he greets me at the door.

"Hi, Etta. You look beautiful." If he realizes I'm wearing the same dress from the Spring Fling he doesn't mention it. I'm sure it's tacky, showing up in the same cocktail dress that he only just saw me in a few weeks ago, but it's the only one that I liked out of the dozen or so dresses hanging in my closet.

"Wow, looks like your mom went all out for this event." I watch as several servers dressed in white went around passing out *hor d'oeuvres*. Somewhere in the back of my mind, I know the distinction between parties that serve appetizers (like pigs in a blanket), versus an event like tonight—this function is totally high class.

Alex snorts. "At a grand a plate, I hope so."

Holy crap! I'm glad I didn't have a drink or I would have choked. A thousand bucks just to eat dinner at the senator's house? This is a little extreme, not to mention way out of my league. So instead of spewing a nonexistent drink, I smooth my dress of imaginary wrinkles out of nervousness.

"Don't freak out. These fundraisers are pretty boring actually. People just come as an excuse to network and drink the free booze," he assures me. "Besides, Jaime is going to be here soon."

Relief floods over me and Alex slips his arm around my waist for added reassurance. He leads me towards the backyard that's been transformed into an outdoor dining area. It looks like a completely different place than when we trashed the place a few days ago. Senator Stewart must have some very big connections that include even the highest power; the weather holds out and it's a beautiful night to hold an outdoor event.

I haven't been here five minutes when Alex abandons me in a crowd full of strangers to assist his mom with the guests. I thought I'd be with him the entire time, not left to my own devices, making conversation with strangers. So while Alex runs off to help his mom, I wander over to the hot buffet. Ahead of me in line are two attractive looking women—who look like they'd be more at home at a fashion show than a political fundraiser. I can't help but overhear as the two women giggle and gossip in front of me. Eavesdropping isn't something I normally do, but with my dad still missing, I've made it my mission to keep my ears open throughout the evening in the hopes of finding information on his whereabouts. I seriously doubt these two models are privy to top secret government intelligence, but it is Washington politics we're talking about after all.

The blonde with the black cocktail dress giggles first. "I hear he's the next up and comer. Something to do with bio-warfare. He's too gorgeous to be a science geek."

"I wonder if he's married?" The other model-like-waif inquires. Her dress looks like its better suited for a teenager, not a woman trying to land a husband.

But the woman in black is determined. "From what I hear, he's single and the most eligible bachelor in Washington. I'm going to introduce myself."

I watch in fascination as the woman in the slinky black dress gets the courage to approach the man standing next to the bar. His back is to us, so don't have a good view of his face, but I'm enthralled by the scene playing out in front of me. I've never seen adults act like high school kids and I have to admit, I'm totally amused.

The woman slinks over the bar and stands patiently as the object of her affection is preoccupied, conversing with some older man. She waits until there's a break in the conversation to make her move. She taps him on his shoulder, which catches his attention and that's when I actually get a full view of his face.

Coal colored eyes that demand to be blue...Cooper!

But something isn't right. He looks...older. I slowly make my way over to the bar in order to get a closer look. Neither the Cooper-look-alike, nor the woman is aware that I'm standing just a few feet away from them. Now I'm able to get a better look at him. There is no doubt in my mind about who he is. Only, he looks to have aged about ten years. What the hell is going on?

"Hey, Etta. There you are." Alex comes over to my side. "I thought I lost you there for a second."

"Oh, hey, yeah. Looks like your mom's event is a big success." I'm a bit distracted by the couple, while trying to talk to Alex at the same time.

Claudia Lefeve

I finally avert my gaze long enough to notice Alex's anxious expression. "Come on, my mom's dying to see you again."

I just hope I don't say the wrong thing in front of the senator. Alex appears oblivious to the situation and seems excited about showing me off. I'm a bit curious to see how the introductions will play out. I know from the journal that Senator Stewart has already met me before and I'm not sure if I'm up for an encore, based on her reception of me the last time we met.

Reluctantly, I allow Alex to drag me away. I take a last glance at alternate-Cooper and the model, but they're gone. Oh well, I'm sure I'll catch up with them later. As we head over to where Alex's mom is holding court, my mind quickly runs over the possible facts about the man I just saw: the man is too old to be Cooper and too young to be his father. After my obligatory meet and greet with the senator, I'm going to find out just who exactly he is.

We approach Alex's mom and I'm a bit embarrassed when Alex interrupts her just to announce my appearance. It seemed silly actually, I doubt she even cares whether or not her son's so-called girlfriend is here, but I can tell it's important to Alex. Although I don't see why, given the way she treated me the night of the Spring Fling.

"Mom." Alex cuts in between his mother and some distinguished looking man. "Etta's here."

"Hello Mrs. Stewart. It's nice to see you again. Thank you for inviting me." I thrust my hand out to shake hers.

Her eyes flinch at my *faux pas*. I realize I addressed her as Mrs. instead of Senator. She recovers quickly and accepts my outstretched hand and shakes it gently. She studies me with cautious eyes and her gaze trails over my dress. Like her son, she doesn't mention the fact that she's previously seen me in the exact same dress only weeks before. "Yes, hello, Etta dear. I'm glad you were able to join us tonight."

"I'm glad I could make it." I hope I'm done speaking to her. I don't know what else to say. "Well, I don't want to intrude any further, so I'll leave you to your guests." That's my signal to Alex that I'm done mingling, while at the same time shooting an apologetic smile at the man we'd so rudely interrupted. I don't even bother to ask about my dad. This certainly isn't the right time to start asking about his whereabouts. Maybe she's not the right person to help me after all.

Alex takes the hint. "Yeah, okay. See you later mom," Alex says, steering me back into the throng of the crowd.

"Where's Jaime? I thought she was supposed to be here by now?" What I really want to do is take Jaime aside and get her opinion on the Cooper look-alike.

"Dunno. She said she'd be coming with her parents. Let's go find her."

We finally spot Jaime hanging out by the oyster shucking table. She sees us approaching and waves us over.

"You actually eat them raw?" I can't imagine eating raw oysters or even cooked oysters for that matter. They looked like slugs. I watch Jaime in fascination as she squeezes off a bit of lemon and adds a dab of cocktail sauce before slurping up one of the slimy creatures from its shell.

"You don't know what you're missing," she says, licking her lips. "You'd like it if you tried it."

"I'll pass." That's just gross. I saw something on the Food Network once that said the slimy things are actually still alive when you eat them.

"Ladies, if you'll excuse me for a moment, I have to go check on the booze. The last time my mom had an event, we ran out of scotch and it wasn't a pretty sight." He takes off in the direction of the house. Is it me, or is he doing his best to ignore me all evening?

Under different circumstances, I would have been annoyed by Alex leaving my side again, but I have Jaime with me now and I'm glad to have a moment alone with her. I quickly fill her in on what I saw earlier. "Let's go find him. I swear, he looks just like him."

She polishes off the last oyster on her plate—ick—and thanks the guy who got stuck with the unfortunate job of shucking and follows me as we go in search of Older Cooper. It doesn't take long to locate him. We find him huddled over in the corner of the yard, alongside what looks to be some very important looking men. Then again, anyone who's over the age of forty looks important to me. Even Jaime's dad is there. The men appear to be in deep conversation.

Jaime pokes me with her elbow. "Oh my gawd, you're right. It's him, only older. What the hell, you think that's his dad?"

"Nah, too young I think. I want to get a closer look at him."

Jaime pulls my arm back in order to stop me. "You can't. What if he recognizes you?"

"Why would he? There's no way it's the same Cooper. He's probably a relative or something. But it's going to kill me not knowing."

"How are you going to get past the old geezers? They look pretty intense."

"I don't know. Look, I'm going to go find the ladies room while we wait for them to stop talking. Wait for me?"

"Yeah, sure. But don't take long."

Um, unlike some other girl I know? "Just wait, okay?" Even though I'm grateful she's here, she really can be a pain sometimes.

The bottom floor half bath is occupied, so I run up to the second floor and thankfully find a bathroom. I'm paranoid about locks—my OCD moment—so I flip the latch a few times to make sure it functions correctly.

After I finish my business, I wash my hands and go to unlock the door. Damn, it's stuck. I double checked the latch and it locked and unlocked earlier with no problems. Why isn't it working now?

Great, now Jaime is going to wander off and I'm going to have to go through the trouble of finding her again. I take a deep breath and try the door knob again. It still won't budge. What am I supposed to do now? I can't just bang on the door without bringing attention to the fact that I'm locked in the senator's bathroom, so I drop the toilet lid down and sit. I need to think. I can always call Alex on my cell, but I'm too embarrassed to tell him I got locked inside the can, not to mention how beyond mortified I'd be if he has to ask his mom for help.

Think Etta! Okay, it's not my first choice, but it'll have to do.

I get up off the toilet seat and back up against the wall, facing the door. I focus my energy on the locking mechanism and try to jiggle it around, using my mind like a bobby pin. Since I can't picture the inside of the lock, I explore the different possibilities: left, right, clockwise, counterclockwise. *Open.*

Just when I start to think it's useless, the knob pops out of the door frame and clanks on the tile floor. Oops. I think I exerted a little too much oomph in my focus. I'm so not telling Alex or his mom who broke their door knob. I'll let them think someone else did it.

Using the circular hole left by the falling knob as a handle, I pull the door open. As I make my exit, I run into someone trying to get in.

"Oh, sorry, I didn't mean to bump into you." Of *course* there's someone waiting outside to witness the door fall apart. Just my luck. I look up to see its Mr. Thornberry, Jaime's dad.

"What happened to the door?" He points to the other half of the broken door knob lying on the floor next to his feet.

He's going to rat me out anyway, since I'm the only possible culprit, so I tell him the truth. "The door got stuck and wouldn't unlock. Guess I tried a little too hard to unlock it."

Jaime's dad still gives me the creeps, just like he did before. No wonder she spends so much time at my house. I'd want to avoid him as much as possible if I were in her shoes.

"I see. And how did you manage to break free?" He tucks his hands under his arms, waiting to hear my explanation.

"A hair clip." I give him my best smile as I slide past him down the hall. "See ya!"

I can't find Jaime fast enough. Now it's time to get a better look at the guy who looks like Coop. While Jaime and I debate whether or not I should approach him, I see him head for the bar. Here's my chance. Jaime stands back as I attempt to make a fool out of myself—again.

"Oh, excuse me," I say, purposely bumping into him. "Is it just alcohol at the bar or do they have sodas too?" I sound so lame, but it's the best I can come up with. Somehow I doubt 'don't I know you from somewhere' will work in this situation.

The Cooper look-alike laughs. "If they serve rum and cokes, I'm sure the bartender has something appropriate for a young lady like yourself."

"Thanks. Hey, are you a politician?"

"I'm a defense contractor actually. And yourself?" I can tell he's just humoring me. He probably thinks I'm cute for trying to flirt with an older man. While the Cooper I know makes me shiver whenever he's near, this guy stops me cold —the bad kind of shivers.

"Oh." I'm not sure what I was expecting, asking him what he does for a living, or even that he'd throw the question right back at me. "I go to Dominion Hall Academy." I check the line and he's one away from reaching the bar. I'm running out of time to ask any more questions. "So, do you have any kids?" Okay, that cinches it. I'm officially a loser. This guy knows I'm certifiably nuts by now. But I have to ask, just in case he is Coop's dad. Maybe he's an older brother or something.

"Uh, no, not that I know of," he chuckles, amused by his own joke. The bartender interrupts, asking to take his drink order, so the man turns his back to me while he orders a scotch on the rocks. Alex wasn't kidding about the scotch.

Drink in hand, he starts to make his way back into the crowd. This is it. "Well, it was nice talking to you. My name is Etta." I stick my hand out, forcing him to reciprocate.

"The pleasure is all mine young lady. Cooper," he shakes my outstretched hand. "Cooper Everett."

I drop his hand and for a moment just stand there gaping at the unoccupied space left by the man who shares the same name as Cooper. I can hear someone in the background.

"Miss? What can I get you?" The bartender asks again.

"Oh, nothing," I start to walk away. "Just my sanity."

Chapter Twenty-Two
Time Travel

Before we left Alex's house last night, Jaime and I had agreed to meet up twenty minutes before physics class. I'm totally behind in my homework and my intention is to ask her for help before class, but after what happened last night, discussion of the mysterious man takes precedence.

"I can't believe that man was Cooper," Jaime says. "It's just not possible. Is it?" She seems genuinely perplexed. I'm glad I had her check him out for herself. If she hadn't, I'd have to wonder if I'm just imagining things.

"It just doesn't make sense. The guy at the bar said he didn't have any kids, but he's the spitting image of him. Not to mention they share the exact same name. I think there's more going on than Cooper's letting on," I admit. At some point I'm going to have to bite the bullet and let Jaime in.

"Why don't you just ask him?" Jaime asks.

"He doesn't always answer his phone and I don't even know where he lives."

Jaime ponders that for a second. "I thought you guys were good friends? He certainly knows how to find you," she points out. "I'm sure he'll show up eventually. He always does."

She's right. Cooper always magically appears whenever I need him most. But given the circumstances, even this is all too bizarre. The man I met at the fundraiser seemed like a nice enough guy, but there was something about him that seemed off. Could he really be Cooper? If alternate realities existed—and I know now that they do—is it possible that it's the same person, only from a different reality? But if that's true, it can only mean one thing.

I know I'm taking a risk by asking, but then again, it's not like I'm actually going to reveal that alternate realities actually exist, so I ask anyway, "Hey Jaime, do you think time travel is possible?"

This strikes her as hilarious. "Where did that come from? No, I don't think it's possible. Why? You think Cooper is from the future or something?"

No, more like the past.

"No," I sigh. Bouncing theories off Jaime probably isn't the brightest idea, but it's not like I can come straight out and ask Cooper about it. At least not until I figure out a reasonable explanation for his look-alike.

"Hey, do you want to sleep over on Friday?" Jaime has already become bored with the conversation and changes the subject.

"I thought you wanted to go hot tubbing in Wintergreen?"

"Yeah, about that. The folks put a kibosh on that one. So you do you want to come over instead?"

Claudia Lefeve

"Like a slumber party?" I've never be to one before. Although technically, having lived at Dominion House with thirty other foster kids was like a perpetual sleepover I couldn't wait to end.

"Sure. You, me, a tub of popcorn, and a couple of chick flicks."

"I'm sure it will be alright with Aunt Maggie." Jaime spends so much time at my house, I figure my aunt will want a break. Maybe this won't be so bad. It will also give me a chance to get to know this Jaime a little better. Besides, a sleepover does sound kinda fun when she puts it that way.

"I'm in," I accept her invitation just as the bell rings, signaling the start of class. Now I just hope Miss Stone doesn't call on me to share last night's homework.

No such luck. If I had the opportunity of taking the course for the whole semester, like the rest of the class, instead of being dumped here the last part of the year, I'm sure I could have figured out the assignment. And of course, Miss Stone decides to call on me to present my circuit diagram. I don't know why they're called simple volt meters, there's nothing simple about them. I slowly make my way up to the front of the classroom and I've got nothing.

"Miss Fleming, please see me after class." I receive a stern look as she allows me to return to my seat.

Great, now I'm possibly facing detention—do they even have detention at a place like this? Or worse yet, additional homework. I sit through the rest of class with my head firmly focused on my desk. I'm afraid that if I look up, Miss Stone will only single me out again and give me her usual scowl.

The bell rings and I watch as everyone exits the classroom. Jaime shoots me a look before she leaves. Now it's just me and Miss Stone. I'm tempted to tell her about my experience with alternate realties for real this time. At the very least, she'll think I'm just unbalanced and let me slide.

"Etta. What seems to be the problem? Your progress has significantly dropped below what is required for this class. This is not the kind of work I expect coming from you. Is there a problem at home I should know about?" For a split second, she actually appears concerned. Then it's gone. "Have you asked your father to help you with your studies?"

"Uh, my dad isn't home at the moment. He's away on business."

She gives me a hard look. "I see. Do you know when he'll be back? I don't want you slipping in class." Her eyes flicker, as if something suddenly occurs to her. "Etta, what lesson did we go over before we broke for winter break?"

Is this a trick question? "I think, well, I—" I lower my head, embarrassed. "I'm sorry Miss Stone. I don't remember." Hell, I don't know why I have to apologize. It's not my fault I don't remember the damn lectures from last fall. I wasn't even here! I raise my head to look back at her.

Her eyes widen. "I see," she says again. "Well, then, I expect you'll make an effort on your assignments the rest of the semester. Is that understood?"

I sigh. "Yeah, I understand."

Claudia Lefeve

Chapter Twenty-Three
My First Slumber Party

My Aunt Maggie thrilled I when I tell her I'm having a slumber party with Jaime. Something about behaving more like a teenager, she says when she gives her permission. She has a point; I never really had much of a real childhood.

I quickly head up to my room to pack a few things for my sleepover. When Jaime first suggested it, I was hesitant, but I'm actually looking forward to it now. I stuff a few items in my bag: pjs, toothbrush and my hair brush. I figure I can just borrow anything else I need. This is actually going to be fun, I tell myself.

Before heading over to Jaime's, I pop in the kitchen to say goodbye. I choke back surprise at seeing my teacher sitting comfortably in the kitchen. Aunt Maggie, the great hostess that she is, has already offered her coffee and homemade scones.

"Miss Stone, what are you doing here?" God, I hope she didn't come by to tell my aunt I'm flunking physics.

"April," she says, turning the stool around in order to address me. "You can call me April."

"Am I in trouble?" I thought our little meeting after class was the end of the discussion. She didn't say anything about coming over to discuss my poor grades.

"Maggie?" Miss Stone turns to my aunt for assistance.

They're on a first name basis?

My aunt tears herself away from the fridge and answers for her. "Honey, this isn't about your studies," she smiles. "I'm well aware of your poor performance, but that's not why she's here. April is your advisor."

Huh? I'm supposed to get private tutoring now? How is this not about my grades? "Can't I just study with Jaime?"

"What? Oh, no. She's not here to mentor you on a scholastic level, April is your advisor. Every beginning traveler has a guide."

Maybe I was too quick to keep Jaime and Alex out of the loop. It turns out everyone knows. I turn to face Miss Stone. "So you knew all this time?"

Miss Stone, uh, April, glances at my aunt for some kind of approval before saying anything. "No. I had my suspicions, but I wasn't positive until this afternoon. When you couldn't tell me last semester's lesson, I realized you were back."

Yeah, yeah, I know, reset memories. I get it. "So what, you've been just waiting around for me?"

"Something like that." You'd think she'd lose the attitude, but she still has that annoyed look on her face. "My assignment, handed down by the Council, was to assume the role as your physics teacher. I've been teaching at Dominion for several years now, wondering if you would ever show up. Now that you have, it's my responsibility to advise you in your role as a traveler."

I'm a traveler? Aunt Maggie didn't mention any of this when she talked about arranging jumps. Is anyone around here going to start telling me the full truth? Full disclosure goes a long way.

To her credit, my aunt looks apologetic. "I only just found out myself. I had no idea that you were marked to be a traveler until April showed up and explained things."

"What about Cooper? Why isn't he my advisor? He's the one who brought me here."

April almost spewed her coffee. "Cooper? That's how you got here?"

"Well, yeah. Don't you know that? I'd think that would be something you'd know if you were my advisor." It feels good being able to stand up to her, now that's she's on my turf.

She straightens herself up, obviously caught off guard. "There was never any definitive information, as to whether or not you'd ever show up. Frankly, I was never pleased with this particular assignment, waiting for a girl who may never return."

It sounds like they just threw her here to sit and wait for me. They probably forgot about her. That's gotta suck. No wonder she always looks at me funny. I'm the reason she got stuck with the loser job of waiting for me.

"Look. I'm tired of all these new revelations about my new life. You two can sit and chat while I'm keeping my plans to hang out with Jaime." I sling my bag over my shoulder. "Aunt Maggie can fill you in on everything, including Cooper."

Before either of them can say a word, I storm out of the kitchen.

It only takes a couple of minutes to reach Jaime's. Even though I lived in this very house as a foster kid, I'm still a little hesitant walking through the door of the Thornberry's. I knock on the door and hear Jaime yell for me to come in.

Jaime squeals when I arrive and leads me up the stairs and announces that we're hanging out in her room. Wow. Her room has a small sitting area that's separate from the main bedroom. This part of the house is new. I guess they did a bit of remodeling here in this reality. She even has a small balcony, complete with a backyard view.

"So what do you want to do first?"

"It's your place, you pick." I take a seat on one of the sitting chairs.

Jaime plants herself on her bed. "Oh, no, this is your night. You need a break from everything that's going on. You've been acting strange the last week. Besides, I promised Maggie that I'd do my best to distract you and give you a night of some good ol' fashioned teenage fun."

I'm not sure if Jaime is talking about my switching realities or the stress I feel over my dad being missing, but I'm touched that she's reaching out to do something nice for me. "Okay, how about a movie?" She did say movies were part of the agenda.

"Perfect! And afterwards we'll do pedicures."

Hopefully it won't get to that point. When she said slumber party, I envisioned us watching movies and gabbing until the wee hours of the morning, but I didn't sign on for pedicures. "Sounds like fun," I lie.

"Hey, can you do me a favor? While I'm setting up the movie, can you make the popcorn? The bag's already in the microwave. All you have to do is hit start. Oh, and the bowl is on the counter."

"Sure." That sounds easy enough. Good thing for me I already know my way around the kitchen.

I make my way down the stairs and find the kitchen easily enough. It's amazing what you remember. The layout was exactly the way it was when I lived here—albeit in another reality—all those years ago. The kitchen isn't as updated as the one over at my house though. Looks like the remodeling started and ended on the second floor. I bet it's because no one spends any time down here. Mrs. Thornberry wasn't much of a homemaker if I recall.

The popcorn finishes popping and I pour it into the bowl, careful not to burn my fingers from the steaming bag. I'm almost out the kitchen when I hear, "Well, hello."

I almost drop the bowl of popcorn. Jaime said her parents were supposed to be at some dinner function. "Oh, hi. I didn't realize you guys were home. Jaime said you two were at a dinner function."

I'm greeted with another one of his creepy smiles. "Actually, the wife is still out. I decided to come home early and spend the evening at home for a change. Is my daughter upstairs?"

I nod as I try to exit the kitchen. I am still embarrassed over the whole bathroom incident at Alex's. Not to mention standing here totally uncomfortable, hanging out in his kitchen making popcorn without Jaime around. "Yeah, we're watching some movies upstairs."

"Well, don't let me keep you," he says, blocking the entryway that leads back into the hallway. "Oh, and Etta, I know it's the weekend, but don't stay up too late."

"Sure," I say, trying to wedge myself between him and the doorframe. I couldn't get out of there fast enough. Then something makes me stop. "Mr. Thornberry, you wouldn't by any chance know when my father is due back would you?" I don't even know if he works closely with my dad or if he even knows him on a personal level, but I have to give it a try. I mean, after all, my dad does contract work for the defense department, right?

His stare makes me regret asking. "No, Etta. I'm sorry," he says. "I wasn't even aware he was out of town. I've been trying to reach him the last couple of days myself."

Uncomfortable once again, I point to the popcorn. "I probably should get back to Jaime. She probably thinks I burned it by now."

"Of course," he says, unblocking the exit from the kitchen. "Have fun."

"Sure."

Three hours, a bowl of popcorn, and ten freshly painted toes later, I lay next to Jaime on the queen bed. I can hear Jaime's rhythmic breathing as I struggle to fall asleep. It's pointless. I'm stuck thinking about April. I guess I'll have to deal with her tomorrow when I get back home.

Just as I'm finally drifting away to sleep, the bedroom door opens. I can hear soft footsteps shuffle along the hard wood floors. It's probably just Jaime coming back from the bathroom, so I don't bother to open my eyes. I don't even remember her getting up. Oh well, no need to alert her to the fact that I am still awake. She'll end up talking to me till dawn if I do.

I feel a small impression in the bed and before I can tell Jaime she's crawling onto the wrong side of the bed, a cold hand clamps over my mouth. There's a slight pinch to my upper right arm and I fight the urge to scream out loud. I try to look over to make sure Jaime's okay, but the hand is so strong it prevents me from moving my head.

"Don't make a sound," a voice whispers.

It's Mr. Thornberry.

My legs thrash against the bed. Within seconds, my body begins to feel heavy and numb. Everything is happening so fast, I don't have time to use my powers. I was caught off guard. Then my mind goes fuzzy.

I'm not having any problems falling asleep now.

Chapter Twenty-Four
Basement Confessions

The last thing I remember is being in Jaime's bed. I don't even know if she's okay. I'm totally disoriented at this point. One minute I'm in her bed and the next, I'm sitting here in the dark. After a few minutes, my eyes adjust to the darkness of the room. I'm in some kind of basement. Two narrow windows sit near the ceiling. They are way too high for me to reach and too small for me to crawl out, even if I can manage to get up there. Since there's no moon tonight, there isn't much light coming through the windows, only a small glimmer coming from the lamp posts.

Afraid to move, I scan the area. Against several storage boxes, I see a dark outline of a person crouching in the shadows in the corner of the room. I just hope it isn't a dead body.

"Etta?" I hear the shadow figure say. This time it isn't Mr. Thornberry.

"Who are you?" There's no chance in hell I'm crawling over there.

"How did you get here?" He asks. He doesn't answer my question.

Now I'm positive it's not Jaime's dad. "That's a good question. Who are you?" I ask again. Maybe he's kidnapped too. If he's stuck here like me, I now have someone willing to help me get out of this. Then again, if he could, he would have already gotten out himself.

The shadowy figure moves in slow determined steps over to the center of the floor where I'm currently standing. I shift further back, but then realize at some point I'll be pinned up against the wall behind me, so I stay where I am. Thinking over my options, I figure I have nothing to lose. "I was at my best friend's house, her dad injects me with some kind of drug, and the next thing I know, I'm stuck here in this basement. Is that what happened to you?"

His footsteps get closer and what little light from the outside lamp posts offers gives me a better view. "Do you know who I am?" He asks.

I stare back at the figure emerging from the shadows. I strain my eyes for a better look at the man. For a split second I fear he isn't real. But he has to be. In my heart I know he's the real deal.

The shadow-man is my dad.

"Is it really you?" I ask.

Over the years, what little recollection I had of my parents slowly faded over time, but seeing my dad again after all these years spark something in me I can't explain. All those lost memories come flooding back.

"Etta," he says with a cracked voice.

I try to reach out to him, but my hand goes right through him. I try to touch him again. Why can't I physically touch him? The drugs that were pumped into me must have numbed my senses. I can't feel a thing. My dad is finally in front of me and I'm not even able to hug him. What's wrong with me?

He didn't seem alarmed over my failure to assume physical contact. "You said you were at your friend's and then you just appeared here? Which friend would that be?"

I nod vigorously. "I don't know what happened exactly. I was at Jaime's. At some point in the middle of the night, her dad comes in the room, subdues me, and bam, here I am. That's the last thing I remember."

"You're not really here," he explains slowly. "I believe you're being held in some other room in this house. I always wondered what other abilities you were capable of. It appears as if you can astral project."

"What? You mean like leaving my body?" Jeez, I wondered what other powers were lurking within me. So that explains the all the dreams I had.

"It's rare, but it seems as if your mind has voluntarily opened itself up to other psionic abilities. I certainly did not induce that in you. But it makes perfect sense." He's getting excited at the prospect. "It's complimentary to your other power. Both psychokinesis and astral projection are governed by the same principle. Not only do you have the ability to move objects, you can project your own body and motion."

I slowly back away from my father, suddenly remembering that he was the one who put me in this situation in the first place: the power of psychokinesis, placing me into a world where I have to fend for myself, and now, the ability to astral project.

"So what does this mean?"

"I don't know, honey," he says, his shoulders slumping.

"How do I get back? Jaime's dad is going to realize I'm not just sleeping." That's how astral projection works right? At least that's the way they portray it on TV.

"You're going to have to snap back to where your body is," he agrees.

I'm a little peeved at my dad for everything that's happened, but he's still my dad. I'd talked myself into thinking he was one of the bad guys for everything that's happened to me because of him. I wasn't prepared to feel genuine love for him. "But I can't just leave you!"

"I'll be alright," he assures me. "Once you get back into your body, you must be very careful. You cannot let him know of this ability. Oliver is already well aware of your telekinetic ability to move objects. He doesn't need to know you can astral project."

Now I'm determined more than ever to get us out of here. "Okay, show me how to get myself back into my body."

"All you have to do is concentrate on the location of your corporeal body. But before you go, I have something to say, as I may not get another chance."

I don't want to hear what he has to say. Not because I don't want to, but it sounds so final, the way he says it. "Don't talk like that. I'll be back to save you."

"Just let me say this," he insists. "I'm sorry, Etta. For everything. It never occurred to me that leaving you in that reality would end up like this."

"Well, it's not like you can see the future." I instantly forgive him.

"But that's where you're wrong. I can."

You'd think with my knowledge of alternate realities and everything that's transpired the last couple of weeks, I'd take this bit of information in stride. I don't. Instead, I just gape at my father.

"You were too young to remember this, but when you were a little girl, I used to take you traveling with me. Your mother often worried about us traipsing around, but you always loved our little adventures."

He's wrong. I do remember. The longer I stand here talking to him, the more it all comes rushing back. I remember being taken to the most extraordinary places: the San Diego Zoo, Buckingham Palace, Niagara Falls, and once, we even explored the Australian outback. Granted, I was only four or five at the time, but having my father right in front of me brings back all those memories—as if our jaunts occurred only yesterday.

"Then the extraordinary happened," he continued. "I realized not only were you able to travel in parallel form, but you had no restrictions with regard to time. Unfortunately, a father's pride got in the way. I made the mistake of telling Oliver about our excursions and your unique ability to time travel. It was enough that he knew you were blessed with the active power of telekinesis, but to be able to glimpse into the future—well that had us both floored."

"That's what your research was about wasn't it? It wasn't about psionics or my ability to move objects. It was time travel." It now makes sense that someone like Mr. Thornberry would be interested in something like time travel. As Secretary of Defense, he can then easily glimpse into the future, or even the past, and mobilize troops knowing in advance who would be victorious.

"Yes. Now, don't misunderstand. Developing powers such as yours is nearly impossible. To be able to recreate a similar portal into the future is what motivated my research from simply jumping realities towards the study of time travel. We've always been able to travel to other universes, but only within the same timeline. So you see, your gift opened up a whole new realm of possibilities."

"So you can manipulate the future," I say solemnly. It always seems to come down to this: power.

"Of course not, on the contrary. That however, is what caused the rift between me and Oliver. He wanted to exploit it, use it to his advantage. While I saw an opportunity for the advancement of science, he viewed it as a means to an end. It was at that moment I decided to send you away. Once you were taken from this reality, his knowledge of you and your abilities would be erased. Unfortunately, now that you've returned, everything has reverted back to its original course."

"How did he figure out I was plucked from this reality into the other?"

"Oliver's a smart man. Apparently he had his ways of keeping track. It's one of the reasons he abducted me in the first place. He wanted me to tell him where I had taken you, in order to bring you back," he explains. "By the way, how *were* you able to return?"

"A guy named Cooper brought me back. He said it was important I come back to this reality."

My father shakes his head. "The Council. I was afraid that would happen. He shouldn't have risked everything to bring you back here, but I'm glad he did. You needed to know the truth. Even though I had you safely hidden, no one was aware of what I had done. Although now I believe Oliver was just as aware."

I'm slowly beginning to understand. "I think I dreamt of my life in the other world. Even though I ceased to exist because I was living another life at Dominion House, when I resumed my place in this world, I found my journal. I'd been dreaming about myself there."

"You, Etta, are a very special girl."

So people keep telling me. But whatever I have to do, I'm ready for it. "Tell me what I need to do to get us out of here," I say.

Chapter Twenty-Five
Everybody Wants to Rule the World

My dad gives me instruction and with enough concentration, I'm able to return to my body. It's a lot like having your mind sucked into a vacuum mixed in with a bad case of vertigo. Astral projection is something I'm definitely going to have to master. I certainly hope the feeling gets better with experience. I'm both happy to be back and sad at having to leave my father in the basement.

Raising my head, I do a quick survey of where I'm being held captive. The room isn't very large, so it must be a small bedroom. Judging from the window, I'm still somewhere on the second floor of the Thornberry house. My arms and legs are bound to a chair.

There's really no point in screaming or making a fuss. I know I'm trapped in here until Oliver comes back. Maybe then I'll be able to get myself out of here. But my mind isn't bound; I can use my powers now that the drugs have worn off.

I sit quietly, running over all the different outcomes that can occur once I get my chance to escape. But I don't have enough time. Oliver enters the room and assesses my condition.

"I see you're awake. You were out for awhile," he informs me.

"Yeah, well, drugs will do that to a girl."

"I'm sure you can appreciate circumstances that require necessary measures," he says.

"Why are you doing this?" I ask, knowing full well he isn't going to tell me anything.

He's now standing a few inches away from me. "Your father did this country a disservice by sending you away."

"A disservice? He's only a scientist."

"Yes, but a scientist with secrets that could have turned this nation into a supreme super power." He keeps talking. His ego can't help himself.

"I thought we already were a super power." I struggle in my chair. Getting him to talk isn't such a bad idea after all. It gives me an opportunity to distract him as I attempt to wiggle out of my bonds.

He takes a step back and paces the room, oblivious to my struggles. "We were well on our way. The path to transforming our military forces was well within our grasp." He pauses to look at me. "All we were missing was a little foresight and power."

"What are you talking about?" This conversation is nuttier than when Cooper tried to convince me that alternate realities existed. This guy is talking about taking over the world. In short, he's totally crazy.

"Your father holds the research that could turn young soldiers into fighting machines. All he had to do was turn

Claudia Lefeve

over his research and we'd be in a position to win any war. With his serum, normal teenage boys can be manipulated to control and destroy the enemy. And being able to predict the future, well, that would set us over the top."

The visual invokes an inner fear within. He's talking about building an army of psychic psychotic youth. He wants to reduce my dad's life work into turning our country into a dystopian society with a lobotomized military. "You're crazy."

Thornberry ignores me. "But all is not lost. Now I have you. I've been waiting for you to come back. Oh, don't look so surprised," he says, noting my expression. "Not everyone was blind to the changes in this reality once you returned. I kept copious records and read them every day. A reminder of what to expect should you ever return. I know full well what it was like before you took your leave in this world, just as well as my understanding of the world that could have been.

"Do you recall your little restroom incident at Senator Stewart's? I had to be sure it was you, so I locked you in. Think of it as a small test. I was pleased to see you had command of your powers. Thank you for obliging me."

I knew I should have just called Alex to get me out of the bathroom. In the end, all I did was tip him off. "My dad isn't going to help you now, so why don't you just let us go."

Oliver stops pacing and returns to where I'm seated. He strokes my cheek. "I wouldn't be so sure of that. You see, I've been doing a little experimenting on my own." His smugness is making me sick. "All I need is you."

Let me go.

Oliver takes a cautionary step back as I internally commanded him to release me.

Let me go.

He takes another step back, getting closer to the door.

"I know what you're doing and it won't work...I came prepared. I'll be back." With that, he exits the room.

I remain motionless in the chair and cry. Oliver Thornberry isn't as easy to manipulate as the butterflies in my backyard. I'm just going to have to figure out another way to get me out of here.

That's when it dawns on me. Cooper! If anyone can get me and my dad out of here, it's him. I slowly repeat the ritual my father showed me before I left him. Breathe and think of the place or person I want to be with.

⚛

"Etta! What are you going here?" Cooper is momentarily stunned to see me standing in front of him. "More importantly, how did you get here?"

I find Cooper working in some kind of old dilapidated office building. It's obvious I interrupted him while he was working. Who works in the middle of the night? Not to mention working in a place like this. He never mentioned what he did for a living, other than bringing back teenage girls from alternate dimensions, but this isn't the appropriate time to ask.

"I'm not really sure." I quickly explain my newfound ability to astral project and how I found my father. "You have to help us get out of there."

"You can astral project? You never told me that," he says, still in awe of my presence.

"Of course I haven't. How could I? I just found out. So are you going to help us or not."

"I'll be right over," he says, not wasting any time. "Do you know how to astral back?"

"Yeah, I think I can do it again. Just hurry!"

⚛

My eyes pop open as I take in a deep breath. The ride back into my corporeal body isn't as bad the second time around. As my body begins to adjust, I strain my ears in order to make sure I don't miss Cooper's arrival. I don't even know how far away he is. When I astral projected to him, it never occurred to me to ask him where he was.

The minutes that tick by are endless. Where the hell is he? Surely he can't be that far away. Worry begins to set in. My fear is that any second now, Oliver will return, and move me from my present location before Cooper has a chance to find me.

I hear the door knob jiggle. I'm prepared to shove Oliver out the door with my mind the second he sets foot over the threshold. Only it's not him. Cooper bursts through the door with my father not far behind.

"Where's Oliver?"

"There's no one in the house," Cooper says, untying the knots that bound me to the chair. "After I went to get your father, we did a thorough search of the house."

As I'm released from the binds, I look over to my father. "Dad, are you alright?"

"I'm fine." He turns to Cooper, "I'm not sure what you're planning, or how you knew where to find us, but thank you for coming."

Cooper's scent tickles my senses as he unbinds me from the chair—licorice and cloves. Even after being rescued from a hostage situation, he still manages to give me goose bumps. I hope he didn't notice them when he was untying me.

"What about Jaime? Is she safe? Where is she?" She's my best friend and I don't care if her dad went all psycho on me. All I care about is her safety.

"If she was here, she isn't anymore. He must have taken the family with him," Cooper says.

I'm positive Jaime had nothing to do with her dad abducting me, but there's a little part of me that can't help but wonder what role she played by asking me over in the first place. Could she have known that inviting me over would put me in danger? I momentarily push those thoughts from my mind, as I focus my attention on the two most important men in my life.

Chapter Twenty-Six
Mobilize and Strike

Cooper was floored. He still didn't understand how Etta was able to astral project to where he was. It was something he, nor the Council, expected. Of everything they knew about Etta, they were not aware that she had the ability to astral project.

What he wasn't surprised over was the fact that Oliver had gotten around to figuring out Etta was back in his world. It was expected and it was only a matter of time before he caught up with her. Cooper only wished he had prepared Etta better. Then again, she seemed to be doing just fine under the circumstances.

Cooper picks up his cell phone and called one of his most trusted operatives.

"You need to get over the Thornberry household immediately. No, not this one, the Etta reality. Do a clean sweep of the house. I want Oliver off the property. Do whatever you have to."

He listened to the voice on the other end of the line as he himself prepared to travel over to the Thornberry residence. "No, don't worry about that. She'll be out of it for awhile. Just get there as fast as you can."

Even though Cooper was taken aback by Etta's new abilities, he had a pretty good idea of how it worked. If he was right, astral traveling left a person in a deep sleep after returning to their corporeal body; it was the body's way of recuperating. Upon waking, the person would feel as though the trip back was instantaneous.

Knowing this, he needed someone to jump over to Etta's reality to buy him some time. He had to warn the Council that Oliver had Etta captive in order to make all the necessary preparations. His operative would ensure Oliver didn't harm Etta in the meantime.

In a way, Cooper was glad Oliver had finally made his move. Now they were able to mobilize their revolt against his regime here in this reality. While Oliver was aware of Etta and her powers, he didn't know about the Council and everything that has occurred here in this world.

In Cooper's reality, Colonel Thornberry must be stopped.

Chapter Twenty-Seven
Family

Aunt Maggie insists that everyone settle in the kitchen while she makes a fresh pot of coffee. It's obvious she's beside herself about agreeing to let me spend the night over at Jaime's. I reassure her that Oliver would have gotten to me eventually. Then she makes a quick call to April, asking her to come over immediately.

Now that everyone is here, it's a full house: me, Aunt Maggie, Cooper, dad, and April. We all gather around the kitchen table. Despite everything that's happened the last couple of hours, I look around the table and I'm floored over with emotion. I realize that I'm happy for the first time in my life. Here I am, surrounded by people who care about me—well, the jury's still out on April. She still looks annoyed.

It's clear no one wants to be the first to speak up, so I go first. "Am I finally going to get some answers around here?"

"I suppose I owe you an explanation," my father starts off. "But first, I'd like to hear from this young man. Why did you bring my daughter back?"

Cooper clears his throat. "I'm a traveler sir and yes, the Council is responsible for her return. Oliver kicked off a chain of events that made it imperative that I bring Etta back. Without her, we have no chance in changing the course of events."

"What do you mean, without me?" I ask.

"Let me start of by saying that when the Council decided to bring you back, it never occurred to them that you would be in any real danger here in this reality," Cooper began. "In my reality, Oliver succeeds in using your powers to his advantage. That's why it was important for us to have you back here."

"So what is Etta's role in all this?" My father, with good reason, seems genuinely concerned.

Cooper looks over at me and takes in a deep breath. "Well, sir, Etta is the leader of the Council and—"

"Wait, hold up there," my father interrupts. "Now, I'm very familiar with the Council and Etta is certainly not—"

Now it's my turn to interrupt. "What's the Council?"

Before my father can interrupt, Cooper explains, "They are the leaders of the rebellion against Thornberry."

"And I'm their leader?" I ask.

"Yes," Cooper says. "Without you here in this reality, you never find out about Oliver and help lead the resistance against him in our dimension."

"Wicked." It's kinda scary, but cool to find out your the head of a council of travelers. "Why me?"

Cooper hesitates. "Because you feel responsible."

I guess he doesn't really have to explain further. I suppose I would feel guilty if I was the cause of Oliver's power trip.

My dad shakes his head. "I'll admit I messed up when it came to my research and how best to protect it. But my biggest failure is with regard to you Etta," he says. "You shouldn't have to carry the burden for my mistakes."

"Well, after everything that went on this last week, I'm just glad I'm back, no matter how or why I got here. I still don't understand everything that's happened or is supposed to happen, but I have a family now," I reassure them. I look over at Maggie and I can see tears in her eyes. I'm pretty sure she's happy to have me back as well.

"Where do you suppose Oliver went? Surely he didn't just abandon his plan to take advantage of Etta." April finally contributes something to the conversation.

I shudder at the thought of Oliver using me for his military experiments. But it must happen or Cooper and the Council wouldn't have risked everything to bring me back. And to think he was once my foster dad. Did he have similar goals in that reality? It's doubtful or he never would have thrown me back to the system. Joke's on him.

"What about Jaime?" I refuse to believe that she has anything to do with Thornberry's twisted plan. Wherever they were, I only hope she's safe.

"I don't know honey. But I have a feeling we haven't heard the last of Oliver," my father says.

Aunt Maggie has kept silent ever since we arrived back at the house. I'm not sure if it's because she's confused, still kicking herself for letting me go to Jaime's in the first place, or if she's just giving everyone the silent treatment for what could have happened to me.

"I think it's time we all went to bed," she finally says. "Cooper...April, you two are welcome to use the guest bedrooms."

"Thanks," Cooper says.

"Yes, thank you Maggie. I don't think I want to drive back home at this hour of the night," April says.

"Wonderful. Then it's settled. We can talk more in the morning. I'll whip up some blueberry pancakes," Aunt Maggie offers.

Once everyone said their goodnights and retired for the night, I meet Cooper outside on the deck. "Guess I need a bit more practice using my powers," I joke.

Cooper smiles. "I think you did great under the circumstances. Astral projection? You even impressed me."

I can feel myself blush. "I guess that means you won't be coming around here anymore. I mean, now that April is here to guide me and all."

"I wouldn't be too sure of that. I still need your help," he says. "There's something I didn't want to mention in front of everyone and I think you should know."

This doesn't sound like something I want to hear, so I brace myself for the worst. "I'm listening."

"When you came looking for me, you didn't just astral project to where I was. You projected yourself to <u>when</u> I was."

"What? You mean I—"

"You didn't just travel on an astral level without using a portal, which is an amazing feat in itself, but what I'm trying to say is, you astraled in time."

Holy crap! Dad said I had the ability to time travel, but I didn't think that meant being able to do it in astral form.

"Just who exactly are you Coop? You're starting to freak me out."

"Let's just say I have a vested interest in your well being."

"You knew all along that Oliver was involved from the start didn't you?"

"Yes. That's why I stuck around to help you. I didn't want to tip you off about his intentions, as it could jeopardize your father's safety."

"You could have said something." I probably wouldn't have gotten anywhere near the Thornberry residence had I known.

"I could have. But the less you knew, the better. I couldn't risk you doing something foolish if you knew that Oliver was the one responsible for you father's disappearance. He's a dangerous man Etta."

"Don't I know it," I say, rubbing my wrists were I had been bound. Suddenly, I remember the Cooper look-alike. He had been talking with Oliver at the senator's party. "Hey, what about the fundraiser when I saw you looking all old. Did he know who I was?"

Cooper just grins. "No. The man you saw at Stewart's fundraiser had no idea who you were or how important you are to me." He takes a step closer to me. "What if I were to tell you that I only agreed to help you in order to satisfy a self-serving purpose? That is wasn't only to ensure you take over as Council leader."

"I'd tell you to get lost." I don't want to hear that Cooper only helped me because he stands to gain something. I'm already falling for him. The last thing I want to know is that the feeling isn't mutual. I'm just a dumb school girl with a crush.

"And I'd deserve that no doubt," he says. "But what if...what if, I were to tell you that by Victor sending you away, it set off another chain of events."

"What else changed? You only told me that it messed up the timeline and you had to make it right so I can help lead the rebellion," I insist.

"Guilty."

"And when I came back and you sensed I was in danger again, you intervened," I go on.

"Correct."

Nothing was making any sense at this point. "So that man at the fundraiser. That was you."

"Yes and no. He is the version of me in this reality."

I knew it! "You're from the past aren't you?"

"Yes, but that's a conversation for another day." He moves in even closer.

I ignore that last comment for the moment. One of these days he's going to tell me his whole story. "Now why would you do all that just for me? Of what importance can I possibly have other than being leader of the Council?"

Cooper pulls me towards him and whispers in my ear. "Because Etta, darlin'. You're my wife."

I look down, where his hand rests on my shoulder, and for the first time, I notice the shiny silver band on his left hand.

*****

Look for Book 2 in the Travelers Series, PARADOX
Now Available

Acknowledgments

There are so many fabulous folks I wish to thank. First, to my wonderful editor and friend, Stacey Turner, who was gentle and patient with me during the editing process. My best friend Charisse Berree, who not only took the time to read my rough draft, but as a social worker, provided her expertise on the foster care system in Virginia. Anything that is wrong or misrepresented is totally my doing, not hers. Special thanks to Shari Emerson, fellow writer and my biggest cheerleader. Without her insights and support, I don't know what I'd do without her. Of course, special thanks go out to my dad (and former physics teacher) who let me bounce ideas off him regarding worm holes and physics assignments. To my husband, chef extraordinaire, who inspired all of Aunt Maggie's culinary creations and who gave me a full lesson on oysters and shellfish. And lastly, all my other wonderful beta readers who were not only supportive, but generous with their comments and input.

About the Author

Claudia Lefeve was born and raised in the Gulf Coast border town of Brownsville, Texas and currently resides in Northern Virginia with her husband and two dogs.

For more information about the author, please visit www.claudialefeve.com

Continue reading for a sneak peek at PARADOX
Book 2 of the Travelers Series

Everything is predestined.

Etta is slowly readjusting to life in her new reality, while still recovering from the shock over the news regarding her relationship with Cooper.

While learning more about her role as leader of the Council, she soon discovers that her future is linked to the five extraordinary individuals she must recruit in order to ensure her destiny.

Nothing is as it seems, as rivals become allies and friends become the enemy.

Chapter One
Here Comes the Bride

I can't help but continue to gawk at the simple silver ring displayed on his left hand. Is he freaking kidding me? I can pretend all I want, but I know I heard Cooper correctly, the ring on his finger is proof enough. I'm his wife.

After revealing the big news, neither one of us have bothered to move from our spot on the outdoor deck. It's one of my favorite areas in the house, but it's also the stage for surprises and secrets. As of late, it appears to be the setting for all my private conversations with Cooper. Some of the moments we've shared I've enjoyed, while others, like the bombshell he just dropped, is enough to make my heart race.

I stop staring at his ring long enough to glance up at the sky above, remembering all the times I used to gaze up to view the stars and dream about belonging to a family. Now, not only have I been reunited with my family, but I have a husband to boot. Tonight, the moon is barely a sliver, peeking through the mist of clouds rolling in. It'll be few more weeks before it's a true full moon, but for now the backyard remains dark, so I can't really see Cooper's expression as I look back at him.

"I'm what?" I say, taking my time to comprehend his doozy of an announcement. In the last week, I'd been given a crash course into the history that is my life: the source of my telekinetic powers, having the ability to jump between realities, finding out I can also astral project, not only in the present, but through time. But this little tidbit of information is like a sucker punch to the gut. I can hardly breathe.

I remove myself from Cooper's hold and take a step back. "You mean you're married to another version of Etta. Right?" This is the only reasonable explanation I can think of. It has to be. Then again, nothing I've learned this last week has had a rational explanation. First off, I'm not even eighteen, yet here's Cooper talking about marriage. Second, how does this even happen? I mean, I admit to having a small – well, okay, a major crush on Coop, but married? In what reality is it socially acceptable for an almost-eighteen-year-old to be married off?

"No, I'm pretty sure I'm married to you, darlin'." Cooper leans in, closing the gap between us.

This is so not what I expect to hear – still wanting to believe I heard him wrong – and I can tell by the lilt in his twang he's having fun delivering this bit of news. I take another step back, distancing myself from the closeness. "Me, me?" I say, pointing to myself. "Just to be clear, not another version of me?"

"Yes, you." Cooper takes a step forward in my direction, bridging the distance between us again. If the subject weren't so serious, I'd laugh over our fancy footwork. It's almost like dancing the tango, the way we keep stepping back and forth. While I can tell he's secretly enjoying this, his expression is all serious. He's standing dangerously close to me and his familiar scent of licorice and cloves never fails to stir up feelings I'm not quite sure I know how to handle. I'm not very experienced when it comes to sex, so my body is talking a language my mind doesn't comprehend yet.

I push him, as well as the lusty thoughts swirling around in my head, away. "Don't you think we could have gone the rest of the evening without any more surprises?" Just this night alone, I find out my best friend's dad is a psychopathic military dictator in another reality, I'm the leader of some Council set to destroy my best friend's dad, I finally locate *my* dad who'd been kidnapped by my best friend's psychopathic dad, and the icing on the cake: I find out I'm married to Cooper. I feel like the whole twenty-four hours has been like this great big Kansas tornado that's propelled me into a world I'm still desperately trying to figure out.

"Sorry to drop such a bombshell on you." He takes my hand. "Yeah, I heard your thoughts," he says, before I can say that's exactly what I was thinking. "I hope you're not freaked out by all this."

"It's just a lot to think about, that all." I want to ask him all about the specifics, but after the night I've had, I'm just too tired to get into it. "I think I need to go to bed now," I say.

It's like I've been thrust into a haze, trying to escape this perpetual dream I can't seem to wake-up from. Though I'm dying to know more, the thought of a good night's rest is exactly what I need to absorb all the information that's been dumped on me. I'll probably toss and turn all night, but at least I'll have a chance to mull everything over.

"You're probably right. It is getting late and you've had a lot happen to you these last few of hours," he agrees.

The fog clouding my mind disappears for a moment and I instantly regret saying anything at all. I don't really want to go upstairs and "sleep on it." What I really want to do is stay here and talk with Cooper. Every time he leaves, it's like a little bit of me cries out in protest. But I know he's right. Despite my confusion of the night's events and my need to talk this out, I decide it's probably better to just go upstairs and head off to bed. My brain is chock-full of information and I tend to think better right before I fall asleep anyway. Besides, Aunt Maggie invited both Cooper and April to stay the night due to the late hour, so I'm sure I'll have a chance to question him in the morning.

It takes all of two seconds for me to get ready and head downstairs. Taking time to look presentable has never been one of my strong suits, so that's not saying much. I probably could've slept in all morning, if it weren't for the aroma of coffee wafting all the way up to my room. In a flash, I do a half attempt at scrubbing my face and a quick brush of the teeth.

I look over at my closet and decide I'm too hungry to actually make an effort to change into something more presentable. It's Saturday morning, after all. I don't think anyone will be offended if I show up to breakfast in my p.j.'s. I do a double check in the full-length mirror to make sure there aren't any holes or stains on my top before I go barreling down the stairs to get my coffee fix.

If I was only half awake before, courtesy of the coffee alarm, the other smells coming from the kitchen are enough to catapult me into full alertness. My Aunt Maggie certainly outdoes herself this time. She makes good on her promise of blueberry pancakes for breakfast, complete with a heaping side of home fried potatoes and bacon. When does she find the time to cook along with all her other responsibilities? It really is second nature to her to create sinful and gluttonous meals. If I was skinny a week ago, when I first arrived in this reality, I'm filling in nicely now, thanks to the few extra pounds I've put on being exposed to all this food.

It looks like I'm the last one to come down for breakfast. The kitchen looks like a repeat of last night, with everyone having gathered around the kitchen table. All present and accounted for, ready to start the day.

I eye Cooper as I take my seat at the table. Is he going to make the grand announcement about our pending marriage or is he expecting me to? Or was last night's revelation about us being married supposed to be kept secret? He's not returning my stare, but I can tell he knows I'm watching him by the way he's purposely avoiding me. I decide not to say anything about being betrothed in front of everyone and instead, take a heaping helping of potatoes.

"So," I start abruptly. "When do I get to find out about being a traveler?" I know a little bit about traveling from Cooper and my aunt, but I didn't know I actually was one until April, a.k.a. Miss Stone, my physics teacher, came over to the house to tell me she's some kind of assigned advisor to me. She's not one of my favorite people, so imagine my surprise when I found out I'm not only a traveler, but I'm stuck with her as my guide. I don't know what it is about her, but she always gives off the impression she'd rather be somewhere else. There's something about the way she interacts with me that rubs me the wrong way.

April takes this as her cue. "We begin today," she says, after swallowing a big bite of her pancakes.

This soon? She's always so grumpy, I figured she'd have me wait awhile before teaching me the ways of the traveler – like, she knows how much I want to learn about my future, but will purposely delay my instruction just to spite me. I already learned a bit on how to use my telekinetic powers from Cooper and got a brief introduction on astral projection from my dad, but I'm sure there's more to being a traveler than that – like actual traveling to other realities. Still, she looks like the kind of person who'd stall on purpose, just to get back at me for having to wait for my arrival in this reality. Apparently, the other reality sent her here under the guise of my teacher at Dominion Hall Academy. To hear her tell it, she waited for what seemed like forever before Cooper brought me from the hell I once knew as Dominion House for Girls.

"It's Saturday, so I have an extensive two day lesson planned for us," she continues.

Crap. She's going to be harder on me as an advisor than she is as my physics teacher. Somehow I get the feeling this is going to be worse than her delaying my studies. How'd I get stuck with her in the first place? It's like some kind of cosmic joke if you ask me.

"I at least get to finish breakfast, right?" I know I'm not being fair to April, but I don't want her to get the idea that she can push me around.

Aunt Maggie tries to lighten up the mood. "Etta, I'm sure April will be a fantastic advisor." Leave it to my aunt's subtlety to remind me to mind my manners. She's one of the kindest persons I've ever met. When she found out I'd been sent to another reality for most of my life, she welcomed me back with open arms.

"Yeah, sure," I mumble in-between bites of my breakfast. I don't know all the rules that pertain to traveling within alternate realities or time travel, but if I'm the one responsible for sending April here to teach me this stuff, I need to make a mental note to kick myself.

My dad clears his throat, preparing to speak. "So, Cooper, please indulge this old man and tell me more about the Council and how you came about assisting with this rebellion."

It's so weird having breakfast with my dad. I only really met him yesterday when we were both held hostage by Oliver Thornberry, the man who used to be my father's partner and who apparently takes over the world – in another reality, of course. While some of the memories of me and dad are slowly starting to surface, they're merely snippets of events I've forgotten since childhood. The man seated in front of me at the table is more like a stranger to me than a dad. I haven't had a chance to fully consider my feelings towards him. Last night was pretty emotional, being held captive together, but now, I don't know how I really feel about him, now that I know about the major role he played in harboring me in another reality.

Caught off-guard, Cooper does his best to swallow what's left of his food before answering. "Well, sir, it's like I said last night. Etta is the leader of the Council in my reality. In fact, it was her idea to send me back to bring present-day Etta to her true reality. She's the driving force behind our rebellion," he says with a hint of pride. He's not ignoring me anymore, probably because I didn't blab about the being married part, so he's in the clear as far as me spilling the beans.

"Humph, that's not what I've learned about the Council," my dad says.

"The Council is a bit different than the one you probably know about. Then again, I don't know how much you actually know about the Council, sir, but rest assured, we are doing everything we can to put an end to Thornberry and his militia." Cooper says this with such conviction, I look over to my dad to see if he is taking this seriously.

"Nonsense. Oliver has been here this whole time. When would he have had the time to take over another reality?"

Cooper doesn't mean to disrespect my dad, but he smiles at my dad's stubbornness. "Oh, he had plenty of time, sir. By the year 2016, in another reality, Colonel Oliver Thornberry does exactly that."

"That seems awfully fast," I say. How can one guy do all that in just a few years? Thornberry must've had something already in place, seeing he failed to capture me and my powers.

"Yeah, it was. With the information and resources he had, it didn't take long for him to destroy a major part of the other reality. It would've been a lot quicker if he was able to successfully tap into your power."

My dad shifts in his seat. "I still don't understand how all of this came into play. I have refused to participate in any of Oliver's schemes. All the research I had, I destroyed, less he get his hands on them." My father nods his head in my direction. "I sent my only daughter away to ensure he never got the opportunity to use her for his ridiculous plans to take over the world."

"With all due respect sir, his plans were far from ridiculous. What he's done to my world is quite serious," Cooper says. "We don't know how he managed or what information he was able to secure from your past experiments, but whatever he had access to was enough to destroy our home."

My dad is totally being stubborn and I can't blame him. To find out all the precautionary measures you took was a failure can be a pretty tough pill to swallow. While I'm still struggling with the fact he had to send me away, I can almost understand why he did it. Almost.

"If I may speak freely," April started. "Cooper is right. Our world has ceased being inhabitable due to the efforts of Colonel Thornberry. He has reduced our quality of living and has everyone in fear. To what gain, I cannot comprehend, but I believe there is more to Thornberry's agenda we have yet to discover."

"Well, then, perhaps I misjudged the situation. I'll do my best to assist you in any way I can. Although I still don't understand how Etta became a *driving force*, as you so eloquently put it, in your plan of action."

Cooper doesn't say anything for a moment as he considers what my dad said. "Sir, I think you understand more than you are willing to admit."

Whoa. Is he implying my dad knows more than he's letting on? That's a pretty big statement, but I don't say anything. I'll leave it to them to hash things out. I still have things to consider myself.

Like what the hell have I gotten myself into.

Chapter Two
All Systems a Go

The Year 2018
Council Headquarters

While everyone was asleep over at the Fleming house, Cooper took the opportunity to check in with Etta in the other reality. Every time he takes the jump between realities, he's taken aback at how perilous his reality is. Torn and worn from Thornberry's destruction, his heart pangs for the world it used to be. In such a brief period of time, Thornberry managed to reduce his home to chaos. But no matter how perilous his reality is, there's always a reason to go back; his only reason.

He finds Etta working in the warehouse that served as their headquarters. She must have gone straight into defense mode after Oliver's attack on herself from the past. Even though he was well aware of his wife's strength and knew she could take on anything thrown her way, he still felt it was his job to protect her.

Etta didn't even turn to greet him. It's as if she could always sense his presence in the room. "It's started hasn't it?"

"Yeah, darlin'. I'm afraid so. Do we know anything on Thornberry's whereabouts?"

This time, she did turn to address him, "We think he jumped over immediately after being ambushed. As far as we are able to tell, everything is still the same here. If he had gone a different path, I supposed I wouldn't be here, pouring over war tactics and schematics." If Thornberry had changed his path back in 2011, there would be differences in their reality here. The fact that nothing had changed, at least by their estimation, is proof the timeline had not been altered.

"No, I suppose not. And the girl?" By the time he arrived at the Thornberry residence, Cooper realized his daughter, Jaime, has also gone missing. For both her and Etta's sake, he hoped she wasn't in any danger. Even in this time, they still don't know what happened to her. It's as if she somehow got lost in the shuffle within realities.

"No, no word yet." Her eyes softened. "I miss her you know? It's been years since I last saw her...since that night at Thornberry's. And here we are, seven years later and we still have no intelligence as to her whereabouts. So my best guess? Everything goes as planned."

"Well, I suppose that's a good thing. We've plotted and planned for so long, it's nice to know where we stand." Any disruption in the timeline could have been detrimental to their plan of attack. Things would certainly be different and the Council would have had to scramble to come up with a new plan – not that they would know if the timeline of events had been altered, of course.

"Hmm," she murmured. "You informed my past self about us." Etta quietly rose up from her chair and slipped her arms around Cooper. "Did I take it well?" She teased. To her, it seemed like it was just yesterday, Cooper telling her about their marriage. She remembered how scared and excited she was to hear he was more to her than just a man sent to rescue her.

Even though he couldn't see her, with her face nuzzled against his chest, he could feel her smile. "I think she's in denial. But I'm not concerned. I know how it plays out," he said this with a grin of his own.

"You could have waited to tell me you know. You didn't have to spring it on me after a night like that."

He chuckled. "Sorry, I couldn't help myself. Besides, I knew no matter what surprises she," he kisses the top of her head, "I mean, you are dealt with, I'm always positive about us. No timeline or reality can change that."

Etta untangles herself from his embrace and looks at her husband. "You're so sure of that, huh?" Her face showed no emotion, pretending to be annoyed.

"Yup. There's nothing I've ever been more sure of," he said, calling her bluff.

He was rewarded with a smile and the feel of her warm hand as it slipped behind his neck, pulling him closer to her. Their lips touched gently at first, then fervently, as if they could somehow make time stand still, for at any moment, their world could soon collapse.

"Good. 'Cuz I'd have to whip your hide if you ever thought otherwise," Etta finally said, breaking her hold on Cooper. "Now, back to the business end of things, I think it's time to activate the troops."

Chapter Three
The Modern Prometheus

After breakfast, everyone goes their separate ways, which only leaves me and Cooper to clear the table. I'm grateful for the chore, as it gives me an opportunity to bombard him with my usual litany of questions. I'm still having trouble looking him straight in the eye, after what he told me last night about being married, but I still want to take advantage of the time we have together, since I have roughly twenty minutes to freshen-up before my first session with April.

"So you're from the future, huh?" I ask. Over pancakes and bacon, my dad was still apprehensive about the whole "from the future" discussion, so Cooper gave up trying to convince him after awhile. But even if he is from the future, it still doesn't explain why the real Cooper in this reality is older; then he'd be from the past. This truly is going to be a dizzying conversation if he ever gets down to explaining things to me.

"Look, I'll tell you what, I'll finish clearing the table so you can finish getting ready before you meet up with April.

I'll come back when you're done and answer any questions you have," he offers.

"Promise? You aren't exactly known for understanding the concept of full disclose," I argue. When I first met him, he was all half-truths, but when you were brought up thinking you're an orphan and a hunky guy comes along to whisk you away to a whole new world – literally – you're willing to take a few things on faith. Not so much now, I suppose. I want answers and I don't care if he is my boyfriend (he has to be my boyfriend if he's going to be my husband, right?), I'm not going to give him the chance to blow me off anymore.

"I promise." He gives, what I assume, is the Boy Scout honor salute. "Oh, by the way, the pajama's you have on are sexy as hell."

I glance down at my p.j. bottoms. They have cartoony yellow stars and clouds with smiley faces. I can feel my face turn red from total embarrassment. While I made sure my p.j.'s didn't have holes in them, it didn't occur to me to check for the childish factor. How is he ever going to consider me an adult, if I look like a little kid? It's not like I picked these out myself. They just happened to be in my drawers. Maybe this is the catalyst that changes the timeline and we don't get married after all.

He sees my horrified expression. "Ah, I was just kidding around. You look totally cute," he assures me. "Go on, I'll hold the fort down here while you get dressed."

I ignore the last few seconds and pretend he didn't say anything at all. "Okay, well, I'll see you when I'm finished up with April. Hey, how long do you think she's is going to hold me up anyway?" Don't get me wrong, I'm grateful for the instruction, but I have a feeling it's not going to be much fun spending the day with her. If it was up to me, I'd rather keep our relationship strictly academic, as in, within the confines of Dominion Hall Academy – at least there, the bell signals the end of class.

"Don't know, darlin', but try to be cooperative with her. She's here to help you."

"I can't promise anything, but I'll do my best." How can I be cooperative with April when she obviously isn't making an effort. But for Cooper's sake, I'll try. I've always had problem with taking the moral high ground and being the better person. I learned the hard way; you have to fight back when confronted and don't take crap from anyone, or they'll walk all over you. It's a tough way to grow up, but it's all I know.

I head out of the kitchen, leaving Cooper to finish clearing the table. I take a quick glance at the clock on the microwave on my way out. *Great.* I only have about fifteen minutes before I have to meet April and I haven't even gotten out of my stupid happy cloud pajamas.

As much as I'm dreading my meeting with April, I do want to make a good impression. At the very least, to let her know I'm taking her position as my advisor seriously. I hope throwing on a pair of jeans is acceptable for my first session with her. I have no idea what she plans on covering today, but I think jeans are appropriate attire for any given situation. I'm pretty sure she's not expecting me to change into my school uniform.

After another go around of washing my face and a second pass at brushing my teeth, I'm starting to feel a bit more human. I stare at myself in the mirror and take a deep, long, hard look at myself. I don't look like a girl who's just spend the last week adjusting from a life in an alternate universe, nor do I look like a girl who was kidnapped and then rescued the night before. It's just me, the same old Etta, with cheeks slightly pink from scrubbing. I know I've gone through some major life altering events, so maybe the changes are all on the inside.

I stop staring at my mirror image, knowing I have to be downstairs soon. Now, where did I put my jeans from yesterday?

With a few minutes to spare, I hurry down the stairs, taking two steps at a time. If April is anything like she is in class, I know I'll be in big crapola if I'm late for our session. I'm in such a rush I almost eat it on the second to last stair, but I quickly steady myself just before I fall face first onto the main floor.

"Etta, is that you?" I hear my dad's voice coming from his study.

"I'm alright," I shout out, not knowing if he heard me fumble down the stairs. Talk about an embarrassing morning this is turning out to be.

"Can you come in here for a moment?"

"Uh, sure." Well, if I'm running behind, I can just blame it on my dad. There's no way April can fault me for spending quality time with him. While I'm still coming to terms with my feelings toward my dad, I still want to hear him out. He's been absent most of my life, thanks to him, but I'm willing to at least listen to what he has to say.

As I walk into the study, my first instinct is to go directly towards his desk. Only, my dad isn't seated at his desk. I do a quick survey of the room and spot my dad sitting in an old wingback chair in the furthest corner of the room. It's almost like he's hiding from something – or someone.

"Victor?" I was a bit emotional last night, after discovering my dad was locked up in Thornberry's basement, that I immediately began to think of him in terms of my dad. But now, I feel a little uncomfortable about addressing him this way, especially since I hardly know the guy. So, while I think of him in terms of my dad, it's hard saying it out loud for some reason.

"Come, sit next to me," he says, motioning me over to the far end of the study. He doesn't seem to be phased at all that I addressed him by his first name. I guess he understands it might be too soon for me to start referring to him as 'dad'.

From what Cooper implied over breakfast, I have a feeling he know's more than he's letting on, but I'm not going to press the issue. He can either tell me what he knows or I'll get the info out of Cooper. So, whatever it is he's holding back, I'll find out sooner or later. "As much as I hate to say this, I have to go meet – "

He waves his hand, motioning me to sit. "April can wait. What I have to say is important."

I take the seat across from him and try to gauge his expression. He looks rather solemn and sad. This doesn't look good. He better not be prepping himself to drop yet another bombshell. Like, *Hey, guess what? You're not really an only child!* Or, better yet, *Um, this is going to be difficult to say, but we have to send you back to the orphan reality.*

But what actually comes out of his mouth is, "Etta, I'm so sorry."

"For what?" I kinda have an idea of what he's sorry for. He sent me away and while apologies are certainly in order, it may take awhile before I can truly appreciate his obvious regrets about the whole situation. He may appear sorry, but it doesn't mean I have to forgive and forget so soon.

"My goodness, child. For everything." He throws his arms up in frustration. "I never meant for any of this to happen. For my daughter to be exposed to a life in another reality, to find out she's some kind of science experiment, by my own hands no less. No father should have to subject their own child to what I put you through."

"Victor," I cut him off. "You apologized last night, but I would like to know why." What else can I really say? I'm torn between resentment and acceptance. I mean, yeah, my whole life up to this point has been a lie. I have powers I have only yet to understand, but he is my dad after all. All I've ever wanted is to be part of a family and now I have one. Sure, it's like twelve years too late, but I have the rest of my life to spend and get to know my dad and my aunt. It may take some time, but if he can tell me why he felt the need to give me these questionable powers and send me to that horrible reality, I might be able to understand.

He shakes his head. "It will never be alright. What I've done to you and the others wasn't what I wanted my work to be about. My research was supposed to mean something. To help people. Not for power or destruction."

"Yeah, it's pretty crappy to find out you've been a lab rat and then thrust into another reality, but isn't there a way we can fix it? With the others, I mean." I'm referring to the other kids my dad and Oliver used to further their understanding of the science behind psionics, or psychic abilities. That's how I got my powers of telekinesis and astral projection. While I haven't been fully briefed on the specifics of his experiments, he and Thornberry apparently figured out a way to alter the way our brains work by expanding their capabilities through the use of genetic altering drugs, or something like that.

I can tell I struck a nerve. My dad's eyes began to take on a glassy far off look. "You know, for awhile I thought what Oliver and I were doing was for the greater good. I've now come to the realization that what we were doing was nothing short of playing Dr. Frankenstein." A hollow laugh follows the irony of what he just said.

"You know Frankenstein?" I was under the impression the books I grew up with in my orphan reality did not carry over here in this reality. The two worlds are pretty similar, but many of the books and movies I grew-up with don't exist in this reality. Which is a real bummer since I'm a total t.v. freak and can't catch-up on all my favorite shows.

He gives me a look of surprise. "Well, of course. Mary Shelley was one of the finest writers of her time. I am well versed in classic literature within many realities. It is a shame she never got the inspiration to write Frankenstein in this world. From what I understand, she never married Percy Shelley in this reality, in turn, never having had the opportunity to conceive the inspiration for the story. In this reality, Mary Godwin was still an influential writer, but not to the acclaim she achieved in various other realities."

As he gives me a brief history in British Lit, I remember being a little girl, before being sent to live as an orphan, where he would tell me stories about fascinating people and historical events. "You used to tell me stories like this," I say. "I don't remember much before I was sent away, but I recall bits and pieces the more time I spend with you."

"I should never have sent you away." His head drops down. "I should never have done half the things I've done."

It's not much of an explanation, but it'll have to do for now. I'm late for my session with April. "It's okay. We can fix it." I don't know how, but if there's a way I can make things right, I'm going to try.

His gaze is still in some faraway place I probably can never imagine, but I'll let him deal with his own internal demons. I rise up from my chair. "I hate to do this to you, but I gotta go meet April. She's going to kill me if I'm any later," I say as I head out of the study.

I take a last glance back at the brilliant man who is my father. Whatever he's feeling, it looks like it's aged him. Not that I know what he looked like before, but I can tell whatever guilt he's carrying around has defeated him. I'm now more than ever determined to make things right. And unfortunately, the only way to do so is to cooperate and make an effort to listen to everything April has to teach me. She's my advisor and if I want to learn about being a traveler, I guess I have to pay attention to whatever she says. Even if it means being nice.

"You're late." April is already seated at the kitchen counter, looking annoyed.

"Sorry," I mumble. Why does she always make me feel like a total turd? She's a guest in my house, not to mention I'm supposedly her leader in the other reality. Why do I continuously let her treat me like this? I have no control over how she responds to me in the classroom, but this is my house.

I make myself comfortable at the head of the table. Earlier this morning we decided it would be much easier to work in here in the kitchen, closer to the coffee pot. Apparently, coffee is the one thing we share in common. I pour myself a cup from the carafe on the table and wait for her to begin.

She taps her pen against the table, which is totally annoying. "We are wasting valuable time Etta, I hope in the future, you will be mindful of the time," she chides. "I'm not here for myself, but rather for you. It would behoove you to make an effort."

"Sorry," I say again. "So, where do we start? Do we get to focus on my powers? I think I'm getting the hang of the whole telekinesis bit, but the astral projection part is a bit unnerving." My biggest fear is that I astral someplace and I never come back. I had a few years to adjust to being able to move objects with my mind through my powers of telekinesis, even if I didn't understand it at the time, but astral projection is still new to me. I didn't even know I was capable of doing it until I was trapped in Thornberry's house.

April looks at me with her usual demeaning stare and snorts, which I assume is her way of laughing at me. "What makes you think we're going to work on your abilities?"

"But I thought that –"

"We start with the basics. From the beginning. Being a traveler isn't about fancy powers, Etta. It's about learning how to navigate the portal so we don't screw up past, present, and future, not to mention the timelines of other realities."

Okay, I'll give her that. "Aren't they both related though? I mean, my powers and being a traveler?" Isn't that why she's here to guide me? My aunt already showed me how she arranges travels for my through a program she developed for my dad in order to allow him to travel and

Cooper made traveling appear easy. So, why do I need a tutorial if it isn't about my powers?

Another snort. "No. The so-called powers you have are a direct result of the experiments your father conducted. It has nothing to do with being a traveler." She says this with such distain, it's almost as if she's jealous.

If she really wants my powers, she can have them. It's not like I asked for these psionic abilities. Then again, her constant belittling of my abilities makes me wonder if she just thinks I'm a freak.

"So, you don't have any abilities like me or Coop?" April comes from the same reality as Cooper, so I just assumed she had some sort of power like Cooper's telepathy. I don't know if she was part of the drug trials, but it's not a far-fetched assumption.

"Of course not. That would be absurd."

Yeah, she thinks I'm a freak. "You don't have to be all rude about it."

Her lips form a thin grim line. "I'm still your teacher. Some respect would be appreciated."

"Today, you're in my kitchen. Respect goes both ways." I've had enough of her attitude. If I don't stand up to her from now on, she's going to continue to keep treating me like this.

April's eyes turn into slits as she stares at me. "Fair enough. Shall we begin?"

Chapter Four
Past, Present, and Future

Several hours into the mechanics of traveling, I thought I'd never get rid of April. Going over the technical side of traveling isn't what I had in mind when she told me she was sent to guide me. Thankfully, she doesn't over welcome her stay here and finally goes home, but not before she promises to come back tomorrow morning at seven sharp. It was nice of my aunt to extend an invitation to crash here last night, due to all the drama with the kidnapping and all, but two nights in a row is stretching it.

Soon after she leaves, I take a book from my aunts's bookshelf and head outside. Not that I can concentrate enough to read, with all the other pressing matters I have on my mind. Instead, I try to replay everything April and I went over today. I realize I don't remember a thing she said about quarks and portals as I sit here bundled up in front of the outdoor fireplace. It's not unusual for the temperature to drop this time of year, so I'm grateful for the outdoor heat.

"Long day?"

I was so lost in my thoughts, I didn't hear Cooper come out to the back deck.

"Coop! You scared the crap out of me!" I'm only mad for a second, after seeing his sheepish grin. I don't think I'll ever get tired of his smiles.

"Sorry, you looked so peaceful sitting there with that book in your hands, I just couldn't resist. Anything good?" He takes a peek at the title.

"I have no idea." My hand goes straight for the decorative outdoor pillow that lay at my feet and I chuck straight at him. "So not cool, scaring me like that."

He ducks and the pillow narrowly misses him. "Hey, I said I was sorry."

"So," I start, getting down to business. "It looks like you have a lot of explaining to do." There are things he hinted at during breakfast and I'm bound and determined to figure out exactly what those things are. I know my dad isn't going to tell me, so now it's time to execute Plan B – get the scoop from Cooper.

He takes a seat on the edge of the lounge chair. My bare feet come close to touching his thigh, which immediately shoots off waves of nerves in my insides. The seating arrangement seems so intimate, despite how far apart we actually are. I pull my legs up, offering him some more room. My insides are still squishy, like a big pile of mush, and I'm at a loss about how to handle my emotions.

"I guess I do, darlin'." He scoots himself further into the chair and makes himself comfortable. "But first, let me just start off by saying, whatever happens from this point on, I want you to know I'll never leave your side."

Now, my nervous stomach subsides, only to be replaced with a big bad case of the butterflies upon hearing that. After everything I've been through, it feels pretty damn good to hear him say it. "You know, somehow I have a feeling we're in for something big, aren't we?"

He grins and lightly punches me on the leg. "Once again, nothing gets past you, Etta."

"So, come on, give me the run down. You're from the future, the past, and obviously you can time travel. Oh, and let's not forget you're my husband. What else am I missing?"

"Always taking things in stride. That's what I love about you." He says, holding back a laugh, but I can tell from his expression, he's doing his best to get to the point. "Okay, darlin', you want the whole unabridged version? Well, here it is."

I don't move a muscle. *This is it*, I tell myself. He's finally going to tell me something important, something useful to prepare me for the other reality. This has to be better than April's boring ol' lecture. I do my best to keep quiet, allowing Cooper the opportunity to talk. The last thing I want to do is get him all side-tracked on an entirely different topic.

"But, before I get into the sordid details of my life, let's start with you first. Just for fun, why don't you tell me what you think you know of me."

Is he kidding me right now? It's supposed to be him doing the talking and me listening. I manage to hide my frustration. "I don't know Coop. It's your story, your life. Right now, you're the one holding all the cards, while I sit here and try to figure them all out. I was kind of hoping you would spill it and tell me what's going on for once."

"Okay, you're right, that wasn't fair of me. But what I'm trying to do is get you to tell me what you know, in order for me to explain things better. Sometimes when you say things out loud, it's easier to understand. So, without you getting all mad at me again, what do you know about me?"

He does make a valid point, so I'll go along with his silly game. "One, you are not from this reality."

"Good. Go on," he urges.

"Two, you are my husband?" I still have to question this one, but I'll let it go for now.

"Yes, but not until much later," he clarifies. "I'm currently married to you, but we actually don't tie the knot until several years from now. See, isn't this helping?"

I guess, but we haven't gotten very far. "Yeah, I get where you're going with this. Three, the you in this reality is old, but right now, the you in front of me is young."

"Correct. Obviously, I'm from the future, but at the same time I'm from the past," he confirms. "Is this getting confusing yet?"

"A little," I admit. "So, you're still from the future." It's not exactly a question. I think I'm starting to understand.

"See? That's why it helps for you to work with me on this. If I were to tell you my whole life story, you'd be one confused girl."

"I resent that." The last thing I need is Cooper implying I'm a little girl incapable of comprehending what's what. I admit, a lot of what's transpired the last couple of weeks has been a bit tough to figure out, but I'm not a child – morning attire notwithstanding. I'm almost eighteen for crying out loud! Almost old enough to vote and according to him, lead a rebellion. Throw in the fact that I'm his future wife has certainly bumped my feelings for him from school girl crush to developing real feelings for him, which makes all this even worse if he actually does view me as just some kid.

He shoots me a sly smile. "What? Being confused or calling you a girl?" Once again, he's reading my thoughts, which causes me to get frustrated all over again.

"Both." I'm trying hard not to pout, but I know I'm coming off like a spoiled child. Which is exactly what I don't want him to see.

"Ah, come on now darlin', you know I didn't mean it that way."

His impish grin gets me every time. "Fine. Continue."

"So, as I was saying. I'm from another reality, but a past reality. I was pulled from my world by your father and Thornberry when they started conducting their experiments on mind expansion."

"Mind expansion," I repeat. "You mean when they started to mess with our heads, developing these powers, like your telepathy and my telekinesis."

"Exactly. Shortly thereafter, I broke away from their project and sought out to destroy Thornberry. I never went back to the past and instead, integrated myself in the timeline I was brought into. Several years later, which is now the future, I was sent by you to get *you* back on course."

I go back to the reason why he chose to stay in this timeline. "Why not go after Victor too?" I hope he's not leaving anything out to spare my feelings. Even though I just reunited with my dad and am trying to understand his intentions, I can understand if Cooper feels otherwise. I mean, he did experiment with his mind and all.

"Because I came to realize, that while misguided, your father really didn't have an ulterior motive in conducting the drug trials on us. His was truly an endeavor to obtain further research into the unknown field of psionics. Oliver, on the other hand, had plans on using their knowledge to create his own brand of power."

"Which he does in the reality where I become leader of the Council," I finish for him. "And that reality is in the future."

"Yes. All of this occurs in my reality set in the future," he repeats back. "And in that reality, Oliver fashioned himself a Colonel and began rounding troops to do his bidding, by using the same genetic serum that developed our powers."

"Yeah, but for what? Wait, why a Colonel and not a full blown General?" Unfortunately, I had the pleasure of having to endure Thornberry's crazed ramblings about taking over the world with the use of mind controlled soldiers. This is the type of guy that strikes me as the kind of person who'd would reward himself with only the highest of honors.

Cooper laughs. "Because he thinks declaring himself General is tacky. He doesn't want to be compared to as another Napoleon. And to answer your question, he did it for the oldest motive in the book...power."

"I thought the oldest motive in the book was greed?"

"Same difference, but the point is, he has to be stopped."

"But why? Why can't we just leave well enough alone in that reality. I mean, there are hundreds if not thousands of realities where Oliver isn't trying to destroy the world. Isn't it easier to just ignore it and stay here in this reality?"

It's a pretty good one too and with Thornberry out of the picture, this reality is safe.

He considers my reasoning, but shakes his head. "I wish it were that simple, darlin'. Let me ask you this, just how do you suppose we know about all these realities?"

This has to be a trick question. Just when I thought I was done answering his questions in order to get the the heart of the matter. *Oh, I got it!* "Traveling."

"Bingo. That is yet another area we haven't covered yet. Surprisingly enough, travelers and their ability to jump worlds isn't something Thornberry, nor your father, considered until it was too late."

"I'm not following." My father told me last night they also experimented with time travel. It was one of the reasons he split from Thornberry, when he realized his partner wanted to use that knowledge to his advantage.

Cooper has a confused look on his face. "What exactly did April teach you about travelers this morning? She was supposed to go through all that with you."

"Not what I was expecting, that's for sure. She literally gave me a more advanced course in what we already cover in her physics class."

"You mean, April didn't explain to you about travelers?" His eyebrows rise up in confusion.

"Yeah, right," I say, making sure he catches my sarcasm. I told him it wasn't going to work out with April as my advisor. "She basically gave me a rundown of the physics and technology behind inter-dimensional travel." As if being in her class isn't enough, this morning's lecture was basically a more advanced course in quantum mechanics – of which I still know nothing about the subject. I'm not even passing her class.

"While it's essential for you to know how it all works, I'm surprised she didn't get into the history itself," he muses.

"Well, it was totally boring and I'm supposed to meet up with her again tomorrow morning."

Cooper slides in closer. "Well, I guess this means we have some serious tutoring to catch up on."

Tingles rise up from my toes all the way to my head. From the way he says this, I'm thinking he doesn't really mean studying. Cooper pulls in, like he wants to kiss me, then stops short. It's not like the last time when he kissed me and I slapped him. This time I'm actually looking forward to kissing him back. But then, it's like he realizes what's about to happen and changes his mind at the last second.

If this keeps up, we'll never get hitched.

*****

PARADOX is available now in trade paperback and ebook editions.

If you enjoyed the Travelers Series so far, check out
DARKLY BEINGS
a new series by Claudia Lefeve.

New Adult Paranormal

Wyatt McKenna has avoided his hometown for years, until a chance encounter prompts him to return to the small Texas town of Caldero, a place where he prefers to keep the memories of his childhood buried.

Natalie Betancourt is sent to spend the summer with her aunts in Caldero, in an attempt to escape the curse placed by the very priests that have guarded her family's secret for generations.

In a sleepy Southern town where nothing ever happens, Wyatt is charged with changing the course of Natalie's fate and the destiny that awaits them both.

15429615R00148

Made in the USA
Middletown, DE
04 November 2014